HER STEADFAST **HERO**

A BLACK DAWN NOVELLA

BY CAITLYN O'LEARY

SYNOPSIS

EARTHQUAKE!

David Sloane is one of the Army's top investigators. Convinced that two of his own have been framed by the tiny island government of Las Flores, he's determined to do what it takes to prove their innocence. When a major earthquake hits the day he arrives all hell breaks loose.

LOST LOVE

In the midst of chaos, former army nurse Sarah Kyle arrives with Doctor Without Borders. Just as David comes face to face with the woman he's never forgotten, he is tapped to lead a manhunt to capture the dangerous convicts that escaped during the earthquake. These men will stop at nothing to leave the island.

NAVY SEALS

When the hospital is overrun by the most brutal of convicts and an American doctor is held for ransom, the Navy SEAL unit Black Dawn is called in. Can David and Black Dawn rescue Dr. Carys Adams before it is too late? Through all the turmoil will David and Sarah realize that their time has finally come and they were meant to be together?

This is an extended version of the novella 'Her Heart's Protector' from the box-set Cuffed and Claimed. It is a prequel to 'Her Adoring SEAL' book 3 of the Midnight Delta Series.

DEDICATION

To all Who Have Served

CHAPTER ONE

Hot, tired and pissed didn't even come close to covering it. He really didn't give a shit what Ortiz was saying. He got it. The man had just been hired, and then he'd fired half of the department because of corruption. That was his problem. As a member of the US Army Military Police, David's problem was to make sure his two men didn't end up spending the rest of their lives in a Las Flores prison.

Wait a minute.

"Can you repeat that?" David asked the Las Flores Chief of Police.

"In my opinion, your men were in the wrong place at the wrong time. I have one of my questionable officers saying they assaulted him. I'm not buying it. I can't figure out why he'd accuse them, but he does have a broken jaw."

"Fuck. Why isn't that statement in the e-mail my commander sent me?"

"Because I didn't want it in the official report yet. Like I said, I don't trust the little shit. Before a member of the Las Flores Police Department decides to make a report against members of the United States Army, I wanted to make sure I knew everything."

David pulled out his smartphone. "Okay, I only see your write-up of general facts and Rigg's statement. Where is Harrison's statement?" David asked, referring to the other American NCO.

"Harrison isn't talking. We're just getting name, rank, and serial number. This is a...what I think you call...a clusterfuck," Ortiz said the last word in English. "Did I use that word correctly?"

"Yep, you used it correctly," David continued in Spanish. He took another long sip of his coffee so he could take the time to consider all that Ortiz had told him.

"Can I read over your officer's statement? The one that you haven't put into the report."

Ortiz fished his keys out of his pocket, unlocked his desk drawer, pulled out a file, and slid it across the desk toward David.

"I've also included private notes. They outline what I think really happened. I knew you would be here asking questions, and I wanted you up to speed."

Picking up the file, David leaned back to read it.

"Take your time. I know my handwriting isn't the best."

"Isn't he expecting a copy to sign?"

"He's still in the hospital flying high on pain medication. I figure I have another day to stall. I'm hoping you can get Harrison to speak up by then."

David nodded and went back to reading. He went over the information four times since it was in Spanish and he didn't want to miss any nuance, as Spanish wasn't his native language.

"There are enough holes to drive a truck through," he said throwing the report onto the desk.

"That was my take, that's why I included my supposition," Ortiz said.

"You mean to tell me everybody in the bar stood by while two foreigners decided to beat a cop with no provocation? Then there's the part where Harrison picked up the pool cue. I'm sorry, but I've seen the military files of both men. Harrison is bigger than I am. He wouldn't need a weapon to break anyone's jaw."

"The doctors say my man's injury was done by a fist. They are quite adamant in their assessment. So I know he is lying."

"And you're thinking—"

What?

A jerky tremor knocked David off his chair.

Was it a bomb?

The floor shoved him up and vibrated, shaking him. The trembling sensation increased. Increased. *Increased.*

Earthquake!

He needed protection. His chair!

Pulling the tipped over leather chair on top of him, just before the ceiling crashed on top of him, David struggled to stay under the scant protection.

Fuck!

Ow! Goddamit, that hurt.

Plaster and dust swirled in the dim light. When would the earth stop heaving? He heard the annoying sound of faint car alarms ringing.

Who was shrieking? That wasn't him groaning, was it?

"Carmen!" Ortiz shouted hoarsely to the screaming secretary.

The earth wouldn't stop heaving until finally it abruptly stopped.

Pieces of the ceiling continued to thud around him.

He tried to move the chair, but it was stuck.

"Fuck!"

Moving his leg was a bad idea, it hurt like a son of a bitch.

"Sloane?"

"Ortiz? Are you okay?"

"No." Pushing with his shoulder the chair moved a little bit. "I'm bleeding. The window," the man gasped.

The woman's shrieks had gotten softer. David needed to concentrate on Ortiz first. He tried moving his leg again. It hurt, but it wasn't broken. He pushed harder, and the chair finally moved.

Sitting up in the darkness, David felt around and realized that a wooden beam from the ceiling had fallen on his leg. He could move his foot. It hadn't hit his knee, just the upper thigh.

Okay, you can probably walk, so suck it up. Taking a deep breath, he hefted the beam and pulled his leg out from underneath it.

"Damn." He sighed in relief. The leg still hurt, but God, not nearly like it had. David felt around in the dark and realized there were some portions of the debris that was stable enough to stand on. He pushed himself up. Pain zinged, and held him in its grips for long moments. Breathe. One. Two. Three. One foot in front of the other.

"Ortiz, I'm coming for you."

Damn, a flashlight would be welcome. It had been cloudy outside, so only weak light was shining into the room through the broken windows. He stepped carefully around the desk.

"Ortiz?" Please let the man be okay.

He wasn't. He was dead. A large shard of glass had pierced his chest.

David crouched down as best he could, and gently closed the man's eyes so that he was no longer staring at nothing.

"Be well. You were a good man," David whispered. He didn't even know if the man had a family.

David walked to the window and looked out onto the main street.

Jesus. At least half of the buildings were caved in. He thought about the rural areas he had seen when the plane had flown him from Panama. What kind of devastation would they have been through?

He turned from the window toward Carmen's weak cries.

Ortiz had been right; this was a clusterfuck.

* * *

"Carmen said you have to take a break." David looked at the child who was quivering in front of him.

"What?" he wiped the constant stream of sweat off his forehead with the sleeve of his undershirt.

"Here." The kid thrust out a hot can of orange soda. Even though it was liquid, he still gagged as he popped the top and the pungent scent of carbonated orange chemicals assaulted his nostrils. The kid's eyes were avid.

"Do you want some?"

"Carmen said it's for you. She said you should go to the hotel and sleep. I'm supposed to make you." It was clear the thought of him telling the large man to do anything was preposterous.

David thrust the open can at the kid.

"Really, mister?"

"Really. Help yourself." The kid sucked down half the can in one long gulp. When he tried to hand it back, David waved his hand. "Finish it. I like grape soda." The kid nodded and grinned. When he was done, he fished around in the same brown bag that had housed the soda. He pulled out one half eaten candy bar and two unopened nutrition bars.

"Here."

"Thanks, kid." David took the wadded up treats and put them in his pocket. "How is Carmen?"

"Grandma Carmen told us how you saved her. She's supposed to be resting at Mama's house, but she went to work instead."

"Where?" Hell, the police station was in shambles. Where could the old lady be working?

"City Hall." Suddenly David heard a man swear behind him. Turning, he saw three men grabbing a pillar that was too heavy for them.

"Gotta go, kid." He ran towards the men.

CHAPTER TWO

Almost two days without sleep and he was delirious. It was the only thing made any sense.

"I can't be put in charge, Governor. I'm a member of the United States Army. I can't be your chief of police." David gave up trying to stand, and dropped into the chair in front of the lieutenant governor's desk.

"I'm commanding you."

The man had lost his ever loving mind. The 'I'm commanding you' line cinched it.

His island was literally a disaster area. The relief workers were due to land in two hours. Las Flores didn't have an army, they barely had fire and rescue, one hospital, two clinics, and their corrupt police force. The cherry on top was that the prison had suffered major damage, and fifty-three prisoners had escaped.

"Sir–"

"Call me Bernardo," the man interrupted.

David looked at the older man. He was in his early sixties and was clearly exhausted.

"Bernardo, I can't be in charge of your police force."

"You can be in charge of capturing the escaped prisoners. I don't trust that goddamned warden any farther than I can throw him. He probably gave each of the convicts a fucking parting gift."

David choked out a laugh. It felt good and bad. In the last two days, he had found more bodies than he could count. Thank God there had been some people in the rubble that he had been able to save. If he hadn't had those mini-miracles he would have given up.

"Governor," David began.

"Bernardo," the governor corrected.

David gave a weak wave of his hand. "Bernardo, I will help in whatever way I can, but why me?"

"Ortiz is dead. I trusted him. I don't want some military man from Panama coming in and running things. I want you. I've had at least fifteen people tell me about you, including Carmen. She hates everyone, and she thinks you are Superman. I need you."

"He's wrong, I don't think you're superman. I think you're Ironman." The woman called from the reception area.

"Quit eavesdropping, old woman," Bernardo yelled out.

"I wouldn't have to eavesdrop if you would talk louder."

David laughed tiredly. "Look, I can't officially report to you. I can't take orders from you. But I can be here, and you can make a request to my superior for my assistance. I cannot be officially in charge of your men."

Bernardo was easy to read. "But there is nothing stopping me from telling my people to do anything you tell them to do, right?"

"I can't stop you from doing or saying anything, Sir."

And the clusterfuck continues.

* * *

So much for capturing prisoners. It looked like he was going to be everybody's bitch. His commander wanted him to go and meet the Aid Workers before doing anything else. Personally, he thought getting started on the prison break seemed like a much higher priority. The doctors and nurses could surely figure out what needed to be done. Hell, there were more than enough bleeding bodies to go around.

David took a deep breath as the plane began to taxi. His leg was killing him, and he'd only gotten three hours sleep in the last forty-two. Logically, he knew he needed to only meet these people, then he should find someplace to get some shut eye before going to the prison. The fact that he was so pissed off was a sure sign that he was getting close to the end of his rope.

Carlos, one of the few good cops left, had accompanied him and was driving the bus. He was going to take everybody to the hotel where they would have a chance to dump their gear and probably rest before heading to either the hospital or one of the clinics. From what David had been told, a lot of the folks had come from Nigeria.

The door to the airplane opened, and the stairs were pushed up so they could walk down. David took off the miracle sunglasses that had somehow survived the earthquake and watched as the doctors and nurses deplaned. His commander had told him there were going to be thirteen in all. Not nearly enough.

Holy God. He squinted. The hair. The way she was shielding her eyes from the sun. He couldn't get a good look at her because the guy in front of her was tall. David waited until she stepped on the tarmac. He'd recognize the way she walked until the day he died.

Sarah Kyle.

Sarah Marie Kyle.

Captain Sarah Marie Kyle. Only she wasn't in the Army anymore. She wasn't a lot of things anymore. *Cut it out, Sloane.*

"David?" The group was arranged in front of him in a semi-circle, and Sarah walked toward him.

Move you idiot! Say something! Don't stand there with your figurative dick in your hand, looking stupid!

"Hi, Sarah." He gave her a faint smile, then turned to the others. "Hello, everyone. Welcome to Las Flores. Lieutenant Governor Bernardo Oliveras offers his sincere appreciation for your help. He'll be meeting you at the hotel. In the meantime, he sent me. I'm Captain David Sloane, United States Army. I'm going to take you to the hotel where you will be staying. It is a five-star resort built last year on the beach, and it sustained little damage. It has its own sewer system and electrical generators. As a matter of fact, some injured were brought to the hotel because it was in better shape than the hospital."

"I'm Doctor Carys Adams." A petite woman with strawberry blonde hair stepped forward. "Me and most of the others have just come from Nigeria. We got a little bit of sleep on the plane, but I think it would be best if everyone could get about four hours of rest before heading to the hospital. I don't want mistakes made while we're providing care."

"I got plenty of rest," a man with a nasal voice said. His eyes were bloodshot, and if David had to guess, he had also been drinking on the plane. More than one set of eyes rolled.

"Arnie, everyone will go to the hotel and rest. Then we will all go to the hospital as a unit and go over the information and protocols at the same time. Have I made myself clear?" Dr. Adams seemed to grow inches, as her voice turned to ice.

"Carys, they need us," he wheedled. "I don't think people should needlessly suffer because *some* people need sleep." Carys opened her mouth to reply, but before she could say anything, Sarah stepped forward.

"Doctor," she said addressing the belligerent man. "I believe I saw you downing quite a few vodka tonics on the flight over. I think you, more than anyone, require extra rest," Sarah said as she stepped into the doctor's personal space. He flushed a deep red.

"Now that everything is settled, if you will all get on the bus, we can head over to the hotel," David said.

They filed onto the bus, but Sarah held back so that she could get onto the bus last.

"What are you doing here?"

"It's a long story, Sarah."

"Are you staying at the same place we are?"

Did she finally want to see him?

"Yes. I'm staying at the same hotel that they're putting all of you."

"Can I see you?" Solemn gray eyes. They still had the power to take his breath away.

David nodded. She got on the bus, and he followed. He sat up front next to Carlos and watched as she sat on the seat next to Dr. Adams.

* * *

Bernardo was waiting for them at the hotel. He welcomed the men and women from Doctors Without Borders.

"Let me explain the situation," Bernardo began. "The hotel you are staying in has sustained the least amount of damage. It has its own generators and water supply because it was built last year. The city of San Marcos is a disaster. We never had a good land line system, so we depend on cellular phones. We already have our cell towers back up. The city doesn't have electricity, and water is at a premium."

David looked around and saw the aid workers nod. This didn't seem to come as a surprise. Bernardo continued. "On the bright side, our hospital and certain government buildings have generators. The rural areas are in better shape because they never depended on electricity or sewer systems, but many houses have collapsed, and we have a lot of people injured in our countryside. We are burying people as quickly as we're able, but we have over five hundred bodies that still need to be buried."

David watched Sarah take in that last piece of information, even though her face remained impassive, her fists clenched, a sure sign she was upset.

Carys stepped forward.

"Governor, we've dealt with situations like this in the past. We should be able to help you with your crisis. If there are specific things you want us to focus on first, please let us know. Otherwise, we will focus on the injured in the hospital."

"There are two clinics as well. Those will need coverage."

"I will ensure that my personnel provides coverage there as well," she assured him.

Bernardo nodded his head to David, indicating they needed to leave. David took one last look at Sarah, wishing they had a chance to talk, but knowing he had to go.

They went to the prison together for the first time. It was a mess. He'd bet his bottom dollar, his savings account, and his newly restored 1974 Cougar that the warden was corrupt. Only seven prisoners had been caught, and they had nothing to do with the drug trade. Since David was at the prison, he demanded to meet with Riggs and Harrison.

"Why?" Warden Nunez asked. "We're in the middle of an epic crisis. Are only American lives important to you?"

"From what you've told me, Riggs was instrumental in saving four men in the infirmary after it collapsed. I would think you would be grateful to him. As for Harrison, he was in the same cellblock as most of the men who escaped, and he stayed. He chose not to escape. This tells me a lot about the men's character. These are good men who have proven themselves. They are members of the United States Army, and I demand to talk to them. Have I made myself clear?" David was too tired to play any phony diplomatic games. Bernardo was standing beside him. He knew the governor would weigh in if necessary, but it wouldn't be. The warden would cave.

"Follow me," the warden said woodenly.

Bernardo started to follow.

"Governor, I would like to speak to my men in private."

Bernardo looked startled, but then he smiled. "Of course."

The warden led him to a small sour smelling room with a table surrounded by four chairs. Riggs and Harrison were brought in by two guards, they were handcuffed but not shackled.

"My name is Captain David Sloane. I'm a member of Military Police Investigations. I came to Las Flores two days ago because of you two. Things got a little off track."

"It sure as hell did." Harrison put his elbows on the table and rested his head in his hands. "Jesus, I thought when we were brought here it was as bad as it got, and then the earthquake hit. This shit just keeps getting more and more real."

Riggs let out a nervous laugh.

"So you're Robert Harrison, and you're James Riggs?" David pointed to each man in turn.

"I'm Bobby." Harrison held out one hand as best he could in handcuffs. David shook it.

"I'm Jim," Riggs said, doing the same.

"Okay, so Bobby, I know you were only giving name, rank, and serial number. I think I know a little bit of what was going on. The cop that you decked was corrupt. He was probably forcing underage kids to sell drugs for him, and was knocking them around for money, and you got involved trying to protect them."

David watched as both of their mouths fell open.

"I'll take your looks of disbelief as confirmation. Look, I don't have time for the little happy dance we would normally do. We have thousands of people dead. We have a worthless police force that is on the take, probably a corrupt warden, and forty-six prisoners still on the loose. Just tell me what the fuck I need to know to get you guys cleared of the charges."

"It's complicated," Harrison began.

"I'm good at complicated," David responded.

"Some people could get hurt."

"I won't let them," David promised.

"How do you know that? They've already been hurt." Harrison was adamant. He wasn't going to talk, and David needed to convince him.

"I'm not going to tell anyone what you tell me in confidence if I think it will get them into trouble. I promise you. I'm just trying to understand. Your keeping quiet only guarantees that you're going to stay in prison. That helps no one. Trust me, the government has bigger fish to fry right now. So, please, tell me," David coaxed.

"We're staying at this little hotel, down near the beach. This is the second year I've been here." Harrison said.

"It's my first. I came to sketch. Bobby's here because of Lola."

"I want to marry Lola."

David nodded.

"Lola's little brother and her cousin are both thirteen. They've been selling drugs in the capital city, San Marcos. I promised Lola I would get them to stop. When I confronted them, they told me that their boss had been threatening them. He's been saying that he would kill Lola if they didn't do what he told them. I said they should introduce me to him. I didn't realize he was a cop."

"What happened when you were introduced?"

"At first, we weren't. We hung around the bar having a beer. The kids were in the back playing pool. The age rules aren't as strict." Harrison let out a half laugh. "So we're at the bar having a beer and the next thing I know Jim gets hit with a pool cue."

"Was it the cop?"

"No, it was Lola's brother. I turn around, and he's standing there, beaten to shit, blood, tears and snot streaming down his face. I knew it was the drug dealer that had done it to him, and who had made him hit Jim."

"Jim, I assume you're on the ground?"

Jim nodded.

"What did you do, Bobby?"

"I took the cue from Eduardo and put him behind me. I asked who did this. He was crying too hard to tell me.

But up pops Juan, and he points at the cop. He says it was Felix. When I turned to Lola's brother, he nods and points to the cop. He says, 'Yeah, it's Felix.'"

"I confront the asshole."

"What did you say?"

"I ask him if he's the motherfucker who uses children? He takes exception to the way I phrased the question. He pulls his gun, but doesn't point it at me, he points it at Juan. That's when I hit him with everything I had."

"Good for you. Where are the kids now?"

"They're with Lola, at their grandparent's farm in the country. I pray to God they're safe."

"Sounds like you did the right thing." David gave a grim smile.

"Except for assaulting a cop in a foreign country." Harrison said as he sank lower into his chair.

"Well, it seems like you might have a friend in that government."

"Yeah, who?"

"The acting chief of police." This time David's smile wasn't as grim.

CHAPTER THREE

Sarah Kyle. The ash blonde hair with streaks of gold had been a kick in the guts. God just seeing her for five minutes at the airport, and almost five years had been stripped away.

Four years, five months and sixteen days.

What?

Shit, had he been counting?

He hadn't even realized he remembered the date of their last night together, but he did. April seventeenth.

David shoved out of the shower stall and dried himself off. He braced himself on the sink as he examined his thigh. He grinned. This bruise was the winner. Even beat the one he'd had when he fell off his cousin's motorcycle.

He yawned, and went to the bed where he had upended his duffel bag, which contained all of his miracle gear. It still amazed him that it had been totally untouched by falling debris in the earthquake. He snagged his shaving kit and went back into the bathroom so he could brush his teeth and shave. Maybe he would feel human enough to get some sleep.

Since there had been two significant aftershocks, David decided to sleep in sweats instead of naked, in case he needed to get out of bed quick. Same reason his gun belt was on the nightstand. He yawned again. He set his phone for four a.m. His stomach growled as he yawned for the third time. Well, his stomach would just have to damn well wait, now wouldn't it?

He groaned with pleasure as his head hit the pillow. The sheets even smelled good. April seventeenth. It was his last thought as he drifted off to sleep. To dream.

* * *

Four years earlier…

Damn, he was supposed to have four months.

"Face it, Sloane, you're a hot commodity. They're always going to move your ass once you have something slightly under control." Rick loved being right, he'd called it yesterday, and his grin was huge.

"But we don't know if the case is actually going to be closed like I said it would be," David protested to his friend and current partner as they walked down the hallway to the exit.

Rick laughed.

"Quit your damn laughing. How were you so sure yesterday? Why are you laughing anyway?" David demanded as he opened the door, and then grimaced at the rain. It was constant at Fort Lewis. Washington State sure was different than Georgia. At Fort Benning it came down in torrents, this was like being under an actual warm shower. Sarah said it was Mount Rainier giving you a hug.

"I'm laughing because you still don't see yourself clearly. You're good, Sloane, and the brass knows it. When you say a case is coming together, they know it's in the bag."

"Come on, Rick, it's both of us. You're my partner."

Rick snorted. "I'm just along for the ride, and I know it. I'm learning a lot. I don't mind. It's David Sloane and his partner what's his name."

"That's not true," David jumped in.

Rick gave him the side eye.

David sighed.

"David, I was the one who asked to be partnered with you. This last year working with you has been like four normal years on the job. If I have to be in your shadow, it's a small price to pay. So let me continue oh exalted one. You told them the case was almost cleared, so you're on to another assignment."

"It's not even close to being done," David protested.

"Yes, it is. We know Allen is our perp. We know who we have to squeeze. This is something I can finish up. Your part is done," Rick called out as they went to their respective cars.

Fuck!

"I'll see you tomorrow, Sloane." David watched as Rick got into his car. He checked his watch. He had an hour before he was supposed to meet Sarah for dinner, and it was now going to be their last date, instead of their fourth.

Fuck!

* * *

She took a sip of her root beer float, and then looked up at him. "David, why did you want to go somewhere else? I thought you loved the burgers at this place."

"I do. But someplace near the water or downtown Seattle sounded nice."

"We have to be at work tomorrow," she reminded him gently. "If we had done that we would have spent all of our time driving. This way we have more time to talk." Her smile was normally contagious, but he felt time slipping away.

"Hey, what the heck is going on? You haven't been yourself all night. Do I have lettuce in my teeth? Did something go sideways with your case?" She asked both questions in a soft and caring tone. That was Sarah, soft and caring. It must be why she got into nursing in the first place.

"No and no."

"Then what? Something is definitely going on."

"Are you sure this is just our fourth date? You sure have gotten to know me pretty well in a short amount of time." He watched as she sat back from the table, and folded her hands in her lap, her expression going blank.

"I'm sorry, I didn't mean anything bad by that," she said quietly.

What the hell? He'd somehow managed to step on a landmine. He placed his hand on the table, palm up. "Would you give me your hand, Sarah?" She looked at him with her big gray eyes. She bit her lip, he could see both want and hesitancy in her expression. He decided to help.

"Sarah," he said in his command voice. She unclasped her hands and for long moments held her hand over his before it finally came to a soft landing, like a butterfly. Just as carefully, he cupped his fingers around it, showing her she had made the right decision. He watched her and saw her shudder.

"You're right, I'm upset." She tried to jerk her hand away, but he was ready for it, and his hold was gentle but implacable. "I have my orders to leave in the morning."

"Oh no," she said before she could censor herself.

"My feeling exactly. I thought I had at least another month. I actually was counting on four months. This is a complicated case."

Sarah sighed. "That's what happens when you're good at your job."

"You should know."

Her head jerked up.

"Weren't you number one in your class at Beaumont? Don't they want you to re-up with a promotion so you can get more into the administrative side of things?"

"I talked a lot on our last date, didn't I?" She laughed.

"I'm trained to interview people. Plus, I plied you with wine."

"That's why I'm sticking to ice cream this time," she said holding up her root beer float. "As for the job, I'm still de-bating their offer. I love bedside, and it seems to be either or. I wish there was more of a hybrid. But that's not tonight's topic." He watched as her expression turned wistful. "I was really hoping for a chance to get to know you better."

David rubbed his thumb along the sensitive tissue of her palm.

Ah, little nurse, I wanted that time too. He watched as she looked down at their linked hands. She liked being touched. She'd liked the few kisses they'd shared, but there'd been a sense of hesitation to go along with her desire. That's why he hadn't pushed, why he had taken it slow. Damn, he'd been looking forward to finding out the reasons for those barriers, and getting past them.

"David?"

"What, honey?"

"I'm done with dinner. Would you like to have a nightcap at my place?" Her eyes shyly met his. Such a brave girl.

He twined their fingers together and brought her hand to his lips. Her nipples spiked under her soft red sweater. "I would love to see your home."

He threw some bills on the table and helped her out of the high booth.

They got outside the restaurant, and when he started towards the parking lot, she stopped him.

"What?"

"David, are you sure I'm not pushing you into something-"

He pressed his fingertip on her plush lips. His Sarah was always worried that she was making waves.

"I promise you're not pushing me into anything. And I'll take that a step further. I won't be pushing you into anything either."

"I know that," she said in a slightly exasperated tone. "If I didn't you wouldn't be coming home with me."

David walked Sarah to her car and opened the door for her. "I'll follow you," he promised.

"Okay."

A half hour later, he pulled up beside her in the driveway of her house. It was a pretty blue ranch style with a wealth of rhododendron and azalea bushes flourishing in the front yard. It suited her.

"You kept up." She grinned at him. She pushed off her hood and looked up at the moonlit sky. The rain had stopped, and now they were blanketed by a beautiful Pacific Northwest night.

"I'm trained to track people, of course, I could keep up," he said as he pulled the door key from her hands.

"No, you're trained to protect people," she corrected. "You're a protector. I felt it from the first time I saw you in the hallway at the clinic."

"You remember me from then?" he asked as he opened the door for her. She went to go in, but he held her back. "Let me take a quick look, okay?"

She frowned at him, "Why?"

"Humor me, it's what I do."

"My dad was like that." He heard her say as he went into the house. He made a cursory sweep of the interior and ushered her in.

"Your dad did that, huh?"

"He was a cop in Georgia." She smiled as she turned on lights, and set her purse on the counter. He watched as she kicked off her heels and dug her toes into the thick carpet.

"You never told me that before," he said as he watched her stretch her arms. "There's a lot you haven't shared."

"We've been talking about our careers and the base gossip. We would have gotten there eventually." She stopped mid-stretch. "I guess there won't be time for that now," she said biting her lip. She twirled and headed toward her kitchen. He followed.

"What can I get you to drink? Usually, you have bourbon, but I don't have that. I have beer and wine. I think I might have some tequila." David watched as she stood on tiptoe to open a cupboard above her microwave.

"Anything will be fine."

"I want to give you options. I invited you over." She closed the cupboard and turned around to face him. He watched as she bit her lip. She did that whenever she was feeling unsure.

"I'll have whatever you're having, honey. Hell, water's fine by me."

She gave a relieved laugh. "Okay, I'm done being nervous," she promised. "Let me give you a tour."

She slipped by him, and he followed her out of the kitchen into the dining room that opened up into a spacious living room. The centerpiece of the room was a large fireplace made from river rock. On the mantle was a wedding photo, Sarah looked beautiful and so young. The man looked young and handsome in his dress blues.

"That's Matt." Sarah lovingly traced the photo with her fingertips. "He died in Iraq."

"I'm sorry, Sarah." Dammit, it explained so much. He stroked his hand down her arm, and she turned to him with a sad smile.

"It's okay, it's been a long time. I just wish…"

"What, what do you wish?"

"I wish I could have seen what kind of man he would have grown into, you know? Twenty-two is so damn young." She bit her lip.

Twenty-two seemed like a million years ago.

"How long were you together?"

"A little over three years." She let him hold her, then she drew back. "Have I ruined the mood?"

"Tell me what you want."

"For you not to have to leave tomorrow." She said into his chest. Then she gave a light laugh and pushed away. She took her wedding photo and put it on the bookcase, so it was facing away from the room. "I was giving you a tour. This is the living room. What do you think of the fireplace?"

"It's gorgeous. You have a lovely home," David said. He knelt in front of the fireplace to get a fire going.

"Thank you."

He turned and stood up. Despite her promise not to be nervous, he could still hear hints of hesitation in her voice.

"Are you sure you want me here?"

"I think I do." She bit her lip, then shook her head the blonde silk of her hair swinging. "No, I know I do." Her gray eyes pleaded with him to understand. To take control. He gladly obliged.

Reaching up, he trailed his fingers along the fine line of her jaw. "Would it help you to know that I really want to be here and that I value the trust you've given me? I promise to do nothing to abuse it." David watched as tension eased from her features, and she gave him a hesitant smile.

"I know that. If I didn't trust you, you wouldn't be in my house." There was the confident woman he'd seen glimpses of at the clinic. "I just wasn't expecting to have you here so soon," she said softly. Now that was the rub. His pretty nurse was used to taking her time. David found he liked that about her. Her eyes brightened. "Would you like a glass of wine?"

"I would love a glass of wine."

She smiled in relief. "Red or white?"

"Red." She went to the kitchen, and he turned off the overhead light and left them with just the firelight. He'd ditched his shoes by the time she returned holding two glasses.

"I love sitting in front of the fire at night and reading." David could picture her curled up on the sofa, her blonde hair caressed by the firelight.

"What do you like to read?" he asked as he got them situated on the sofa. As soon as she snuggled into her position, he inched closer. He was rewarded with that look of shy pleasure that he was coming to know.

"I read a little bit of everything, but do you want me to be honest?" She looked at him through her gold flecked lashes.

He tipped up her chin. "Always. I'll always want honesty." She swallowed, and nodded.

"Most of the books on my reader are romances. I suppose that makes me kind of frivolous."

"I think that makes you human. Who doesn't want a happily-ever-after?"

"They're rare. Hell, I should know that better than anyone," she whispered.

"All the more reason to desire them." Damn, could he do this? "Sarah," he began.

"David," she interrupted him. "I'm not some young virgin looking for a happily-ever-after. I'm a woman who really desires the man sitting on my sofa."

"That's good, because I really, really desire you." He plucked the glass of wine out of her hand and put it on the coaster on the coffee table. Part of him was pissed he was being reassigned so quickly. He would have preferred to slowly come to know her before getting to this point. But as he pulled her into his arms, he acknowledged that was bullshit.

Settling Sarah against his chest, feeling her nipples pebble against him, he was suddenly glad that his hand had been forced, that he didn't have to wait. Having her close was a gift. Her hands crept upwards until clever fingers worked the top button of his dress shirt loose.

"No," he said, his hands covering hers.

"But I thought…" her voice trailed away.

"We'll get there," he assured her. First, he wanted to make sure she was with him every step of the way. She had been a puzzle all night. Sometimes bold, sometimes shy, always Sarah. Now that he knew about Matt, it all made sense. It was his job to make sure he gathered all those intriguing pieces together and brought her pleasure.

Even before tonight, he'd watched this sweet woman, and noticed certain things. She didn't readily accept kindness; her first inclination was to assume it was a mistake. She was quick to assume she was at fault for things that could never in a million years be her fault.

Time with Matt would probably have helped her overcome those issues, but it had been cut short. Now he was going to be one more man who wasn't going to be able to give her the time she deserved. But by God, he was going to make sure that she remembered everything that went on tonight in a positive light.

"Can I take a kiss?" he asked.

"Take? That's an odd way of putting it."

David quickly changed positions on the sofa so he was lying full length on his back and she was on top of him.

"You trust me, right?"

"Oh yes," her breath broke on the words.

"Then tonight I want an opportunity to take you with me. Take you places that you might not have been before. Take you in my arms and make you mine. Would you allow me to do that? I want to start by taking a kiss. May I?" He watched as she bit her lip. God, he wanted to bite her lip.

Easy Sloane, get permission first.

Eyes wide, she nodded.

David eased his fingers under the silk of her chin length hair and lowered her head to his. Her bottom lip was wet, swollen, and irresistible. He sucked the tempting morsel smiling when he heard her whine. He traced that tempting bit of flesh with his tongue and enjoyed how she opened her mouth for him.

Take it slow.

He slid his tongue into the warmth of her mouth, tasting wine and woman, the woman was by far the sweeter flavor. Her tongue shyly stroked against his, bringing every one of his dominant instincts roaring to life.

Take it slow.

Back and forth, he brushed his thumb against the arch of her jaw, then slowly he moved his other hand down her back, and relished the way she arched into his touch. He pushed his hand under the soft red cashmere and found even softer skin. He drew circles before edging upwards to the clasp of her bra. He traced the line of silk, readying her, not surprised when he felt her tension.

"Easy," he murmured. She breathed in then let it out, melting against him , and he unhooked her bra. Taking his time, he made long, languid sweeps up and down the length of her back. She pushed against his chest.

"Off. I want it off."

David smiled. The little nurse was ready to be taken. He stood up with her still in his arms. "Which way to your bedroom?"

She pointed to the hallway. "Last door on the left. My bed isn't made."

"Honey, we're just going to mess it up anyway." He started down the hall.

He liked the way she smiled. She was getting more comfortable.

"Sarah, I didn't bring anything to protect you. Do you have something?"

She nodded. "I'm a nurse. Are you going to let me down now?" she teased.

"I'm considering it."

He looked around the room, it was soothing tones of blue. It suited her.

David let her slide down his body, lifting her sweater and bra off her body as he went. Pink. He'd wondered. Now he knew her nipples were pink.

"Now you."

"No." She had a lot to learn. "You agreed to be taken." The hesitation was back, but not in a bad way, he saw curiosity. Good.

They were still too new to one another for her to strip in front of him, so he brought her close for another kiss, which was not a hardship. She wrapped her arms around his neck, but he brought them down to her sides.

"David?"

"Taken. Your turn will come later. This is my time to please you." A delightful frown appeared between her eyes, but she put her hands to her sides. Could he get any harder as he saw her hands clench and relax? He traced his fingers from her collar bone to her sternum, over the tips of her breasts, and enjoyed the jerk of response. Then he went further, to the belly button exposed by her low rider jeans. He let his fingers glide across the top of her waistband, watching her tremble.

"Please."

He unbuttoned the top button, then unzipped, and was rewarded with red silk panties. David pushed his fingers in and under. Damn, she was soft and bare, and his smile turned savage as he probed further to find her wet folds.

Honey. It was the perfect word for her. He pulled his fingers out and brought them to his mouth and sucked them in. "I knew you'd taste like honey." Her eyes were wide, just a slight bit of gray rimmed black as she panted.

"Can I touch you yet?" Her voice was breathless.

"No." David bent, and as he helped her step out of her jeans and panties, he took a long lick of her feminine folds and suckled her clit.

"David!" she wailed as she came apart. He grabbed her close and laid her down on the bed.

"Where are the condoms?" he asked as he reached for the bedside drawer.

"Wait, let me," she scrambled to stop him.

Too late.

Score.

He had found Sarah's little assortment of treasure. He pulled out a small vibrator that couldn't come close to matching what they would be working with tonight.

"Too bad we don't have more time," he said regretfully as he placed it back in the nightstand. He pulled out a condom and stood beside the bed. He made short work of stripping, delighting in how she reached for him, but they were still on his program. "Sarah?" he asked.

"Hmmm?" She was in a fog. "Now, I need you now."

"And I'm going to *take* you." He emphasized the word take. "Hands over your head."

"No," she said petulantly. "I want to touch you. I love your chest."

"Next time."

"Now." She pushed out her bottom lip.

It was too much to bear. He swooped down and shackled her wrists. If there were going to be a next time, he would have brought handcuffs. He grabbed her hands in one of his, and pulled them over her head, loving how her breasts were thrust into prominence.

Fuck, this couldn't be the last time!

Sarah undulated, her breasts shimmering, taking all of his attention. Everything but the present moment flew out of his head. He suckled one piece of pink candy and savored the lusciousness of Sarah. The sweetest of all the flavors. She rolled her torso and begged for her other breast to have attention. He plucked and pinched, and she hissed out the word, "Yes."

Over and over, he took, waiting for a sign. At last, her legs were wide open, surrounding his hips.

"Keep your hands where I put them, then you get my cock, do you understand?"

She looked at him in confusion. She canted her hips upwards, trying to capture him, tempt him.

He let go of her hands and went to put on the condom. She leveraged her hands against the headboard, and then used her feet to push high against him.

"Dammit, honey, let me get this on."

She'd tempt a saint. Properly protected, he guided himself into her swollen, wet depths. She damn near strangled him with her need. Had anything ever felt so good?

"Fuck. You're perfect Honey. Squeeze me tighter."

He laughed. She was actually blushing. They were as close as two human beings could be, and she was blushing. She was a fucking delight.

"David," she admonished.

"What? Don't you want to know that your body is perfect?" He thrust deeper. Harder.

She mumbled something into his chest. He cupped her chin and tilted her head so he could see her.

"What did you say?"

"It's you."

He pushed back in, watching her carefully. There, that was the spot. He did it again, and again, rubbing the sweet spot.

"What's me?" he asked softly. His pretty nurse struggled to keep her hands above her head and answer his question.

"You're perfect," she sighed. She was getting close, and he intended to make her fly. He reached his hand between them and found her clit wet and swollen. He circled it as he bent and lapped at one berry tipped nipple. God, which one of them was trembling harder?

"David?"

He pinched. He sucked. He thrust.

She thrashed, her hair flew across the pillow, her moan long and loud.

God, she was beautiful. Sarah came like a wanton, nothing held back. He'd never had such a pure and authentic lover. As her climax shuddered to completion, dazed gray eyes looked up at him.

"Again." Her voice was hoarse, but the demand was clear.

He grinned. He hooked his hand under her arm and brought it up and over his neck. Her smile dazzled. She lifted her other arm and clutched him close. They met for a long kiss.

Just kissing her was enough to make him come. Her release had made her more swollen, and pressing in made his head want to explode, but he'd be damned if she wouldn't come with him. He swept his hand down her back and clutched her ass. She purred and jolted up, slamming their bodies together. He kneaded the lush curves, and she moaned. Wrenching her mouth away from his she gasped, "It's too much."

If she could talk, it wasn't enough. He slowed down, then sped up, ensuring she would never know what to expect. He heard her gasping and grinned.

Ahhh, her nails in his scalp were going to draw blood, and he would happily wear the wounds. As her walls clamped down on his cock, tingles shot down his spine. She was going to kill him, and then she wailed his name, and he shot over the edge, lost in the stormy depths of her gray eyes.

CHAPTER FOUR

Present Day…

It didn't matter what time zone it was. It didn't matter if he'd had three, four, five or six hours of sleep. Four a.m. was an ungodly hour to have to have the alarm wake you. David grabbed his phone and shut it off, wishing the magical, earthquake proof device could make coffee appear.

He pushed out of bed, and the scent of the clean sheets brought his dreams rushing back to him. Four a.m. Would the medical team be asleep? Be at the hospital? Be coming back? Fuck if he knew. Everything was topsy turvy and had been since the fucking earthquake. It was now hour sixty since the earthquake.

He needed to get to the prison. The warden and his men had been woefully lacking in their ability to put together search parties. Hell, they didn't even have protocols in place to handle a prison break!

His phone rang.

"David?"

He suppressed the sarcastic answer. "Yes, Carmen, it's me. What are you doing up so early?"

"The boat arrived. Where are you?" she asked irritably.

Dammit, he'd forgotten. He'd been so focused on getting back to the prison, that he hadn't remembered the shipment of large construction equipment that was scheduled to arrive that morning. The earthquake had damaged nearly all of the island's equipment on various construction sites throughout the countryside.

"Ship. It's a ship. I'm on my way. You aren't at the dock, are you?" Hell, she'd called him yesterday afternoon when he'd been at the prison. Bernardo had put her in charge of coordinating communications between police, fire, and the governor's office. She was perfect. Annoying, but perfect.

"No, I'm not at the dock. I don't drive. They called me. I'm waiting for you in the lobby." He sighed.

"I'll be there in ten minutes."

"Make it five." She hung up.

Despite the fact there were back-up generators in the hotel, David still avoided the elevators. He was close to the first floor when he heard Sarah. He stopped to listen.

"I will have you arrested if I ever see you touch another patient."

"You bitch. You're just a nurse."

"You're a drunk and a junkie. Look at yourself, you can barely stand. I saw you go into that supply closet, and then come out higher than a kite! I'm going to file every report imaginable. When I'm done with you, you won't be able to dispense advice."

He heard a thud. *Fuck!* He jumped down four steps and rounded the corner just in time to see the bastard roll on the ground, Sarah stood over him, fists clenched, and her chest heaving.

"You absolute dolt. What part of former Army did you not comprehend?" She nudged him with her toe and then looked up. "Oh lookie, it's the police."

Dumbass groaned.

"Get up," Sarah growled.

He just moaned.

"I barely tapped him," she said as she looked at David. "He's high. I hauled him out of the clinic we were working at." Despite her brave words, he could see shock was beginning to set in.

"Honey," he started. But she put her hand out and shook her head. Instead, she pointed to the man lying on the floor of the stairwell.

David nodded, and she gave a weak smile of appreciation.

"What's your name, asshole?" David demanded. The man just moaned again. David pulled him up and gave him a shake. "Name!"

"Arnie. Dr. Arnie Stanton," he slurred. Sarah opened the door to the lobby, and David marched the doctor out. He saw Carmen who immediately summed up the situation. She had her phone out in an instant. After she had hung up, she came over to them.

"Carlos will be here in five minutes. I take it this idiot needs to be booked?" David revised his opinion of the older woman for the forty-third time. Once again, he adored Carmen.

"Are you okay, honey?" she asked Sarah.

"I'm fine," came the clipped response.

"You talk to our chief, we'll take care of the trash," the older woman said in a soothing tone.

David looked in amazement as Carlos walked up.

"How did you get here so fast?"

"Carmen wanted a ride to the docks. She said you were taking too long." Okay, now Carmen was annoying him again. David explained the situation about the doctor.

"Do you need me to make a statement?" Sarah asked Carlos.

"I'll take it," David said. "You can take the prisoner to our temporary holding cell, and then take Carmen to the docks."

"Sounds good," Carlos said as he turned to Sarah. "We're going to have a man at the clinic by lunch. We don't want you left undefended."

"We have weapons locked up in our supply cabinet. We're covered."

"That's not good enough, you need to be armed, Sarah," David admonished. He watched her consider what he was saying and she finally nodded. David and Carlos exchanged a smile, then Carlos maneuvered the unsteady doctor out of the hotel, with Carmen following.

David turned to Sarah. "Are you all right?"

"I'm fine, but I need to get back to the clinic. Do you really need to take a statement from me?"

"Let's sit down. They have food rations laid out over there, and I need to grab some before heading out." David indicated the temporary area the hotel management had set up. "What's more, you look like you might fall down."

She took a deep breath. "Sitting sounds good," she admitted.

His hand hovered over her lower back for a moment, and then a spark flared when his palm touched the light cotton covering her skin. Her step hesitated, then she continued toward the dining room that was dimly lit with lanterns. David relaxed when Sarah let him hold out the chair for her.

"I'm going to get a plate of food. There's bananas, oatmeal, and I think they might have some eggs. Can I get you anything?"

"No. I'm too upset to eat."

"Sarah, when was the last time you ate?"

She blew out a breath. "Last night at dinner, before we left for the clinic."

What the hell was she thinking? Why did she think she needed to return?

"I'll be right back." He went to the serving area, filled up two plates, and grabbed two bottles of water. She could eat what she wanted, and whatever she didn't, he'd finish.

She was staring off into space when he returned. He put one of the plates in front of her and she frowned. "I can't eat all of that."

"I'll eat what you don't. I'm a growing boy."

She started to play with her fork, the bruising on her knuckles was clear.

"Dammit, Sarah! You could have been really hurt. What were you thinking being alone with him?"

"I was trying to keep our dirty laundry private."

Food forgotten, David replayed the sounds echoing off the walls of the stairwell. That man could have knocked her head into the iron railings or the cement floor before he'd ever had a chance to reach them. Dammit, he should never have stopped to eavesdrop, he should've immediately gone to her. David gently picked up her wounded hand and brushed his thumb over the bruise.

"He didn't deserve that consideration. You were always too kind."

"I wasn't being kind; I was just trying to maintain our reputation. We suspected some things in Nigeria, but it was like he imploded in the last five days. Carys is going to be so pissed off. Or devastated. Probably both." He felt the fine trembling under his fingers. He wanted to wrap her up in his arms, but she'd made it clear how she'd felt when she froze him out way back when. It was no longer his right, and it killed.

"I respected your request to not keep in touch, even though it was the last thing I wanted. Hell, you never even gave me an answer as to why. Will you tell me now?" Four years, five months and seventeen days later, he wanted to know that answer.

"That's why I wanted to talk to you," she said quietly. "How much time do you have right now?"

"Enough to eat. Enough to make sure you eat."

She looked up at him through her lashes, her fingers tightening in his hand and sighed. "Me too, I have to get back to the clinic."

"Bullshit," he growled. "You've already been there for ten hours, and you intend to go back?"

"David, I'm used to twenty hour shifts. It's not good out there. Right now the local doctor needed some time with his family. We promised to cover for him until tonight. I shouldn't even be taking this time." Her eyes pleaded with him to understand.

David knew exactly what she was talking about. Hell, it was the same reason he was running on fumes. "It's a deal."

She brightened.

He held up his other hand. "On the condition that you eat everything on your plate." She rolled her eyes and he continued. "Once you're done, I'll drive you. We'll have some time to talk that way. Deal?" He let go of her hand and gave her a fork.

"So you're still pushy?" she asked.

"Yep." He watched as she switched hands, and proceeded to eat with her left hand. Damn, she was right handed. She had to be hurting pretty badly.

They ate in silence. She was obviously hungry because he watched her finish everything on her plate.

Apparently, she's not the only one hungry, Sloane.

God, she had the prettiest mouth. He didn't taste anything he ate. He was too busy staring at every morsel passing her lips.

"David?"

"I'm sorry, what did you say?"

"I asked what brought you to Las Flores. It seemed odd that an Army MP would be here."

"I got here the day of the earthquake. Two NCO's were charged with assaulting a local police officer. There was also a rumor of drug possession. I came here to sort things out, and before I could talk to them, the quake hit." He looked at her plate, and then his, they were wiped clean. "Do you want me to get more?"

"I couldn't possibly eat another bite. What about you?"

"I really don't have time. I'll just grab a couple of biscuits and some fruit to take with me."

She laughed.

"What?"

"I always loved your appetite. I'm glad to see it hasn't changed."

"Oh, it hasn't changed," he said softly as he pulled out her chair.

Then he cursed himself. Dammit man, she was just assaulted, the last thing she needed was some man coming onto her.

"Sarah, I'm sorry. Look, you need someone coming onto you right now like you need a hole in the head. I wasn't thinking."

She turned and put her hand on his shoulder and looked him dead in the eye. "You're right David. If some unknown man made an overture right now, it would freak me out. But it's you, so it's okay. You've always made me feel protected."

"Thank you for that." He needed answers. It was still dark, and he took her arm as they went to the truck he was driving.

Once they were on the road, silence filled the truck.

"Sarah."

"David."

They both chuckled, as they said one another's names in unison.

"You go first," David said.

"I owe you an explanation. That's why I wanted to talk." A profound sense of relief roared through him.

"I couldn't bear to talk to you back then. It would have been too much… Too little."

Well, that cleared up nothing.

"I don't understand."

"Carys and I had been friends forever. She had been asking me to join her at Doctors Without Borders for years. After you left, I finally made the decision to do it."

"That's a huge step? You resigned your commission and uprooted yourself almost overnight. Then you never took my calls or answered my e-mails. Why? You scared the piss out of me, Woman. I had to pull in favors to find out what had happened."

"I was fine."

"Sarah, the woman I met, the woman I had in my arms, wouldn't have pulled a disappearing act unless she was in distress. I needed to check up on you."

He looked ahead. There was a spot. The truck bumped over ruts and rubble before he pulled to a stop.

David unbuckled his seatbelt, then hers, and scooched over so they were side by side on the bench seat.

"Can you tell me about it?"

"I don't know why I thought smart and perceptive were attractive traits in a man." She sighed.

"It was because of me, wasn't it?"

"No," she said at the same time that she nodded. She obviously didn't know she had just admitted it *was* because of him.

"Ah, honey. I'm so sorry."

"Why? You didn't do anything."

"I left," he said quietly. He had left, just like Matt. He might not have died, but he was another man who had abandoned her.

"I was a big girl. You'd made no promises." Her voice was so quiet, her chin trembled. His heart ached.

"I'm so sorry," he said again. And he was. If he could kick his own ass, he would. "But why didn't you take my calls?"

"Do you want me to be honest?" He remembered that question from that night. He answered it the same way.

"I'll always want you to be honest."

"I ended up wanting more than I should have. That was on me. We agreed it was just that night. I knew better. I couldn't have kept it light and breezy, so I cut off all communication. It was for the best." She looked down at her hands and mumbled, "I'm sorry."

He pulled her into his arms. Considering the fact, he remembered the exact date, April seventeenth, his heart had been invested as deeply as hers had.

"I'm sorry, Honey," he said as he cupped her cheek, relishing the feel of the soft silk of her hair caressing his knuckles. "I never meant to hurt you. But I'm not sorry for our time together, and I'm sure as hell not sorry for that night. You've haunted my dreams. I just feel like crap that I made you pull up roots and give up your career."

"There's nothing to be sorry about. I made the right decision. I've been so happy with DWB. Carys had been a dream to work with these last few years. I'm glad I did it."

"You've accomplished some amazing things. I read that article where you worked with the Liberian government to set up clinics. I was so proud of you."

She blushed, and pushed her face against his chest.

"So you checked up on me, huh."

"Not as often as I should have. I should have chased after you. But after that last e-mail went unopened, I got the message."

"I'm so sorry David. I didn't want to start something that I knew we couldn't finish. I was committed to DWB. You would have been too big of a temptation."

"Was?"

"I'm getting tired. I'm considering coming home. I've had a couple of offers."

"Home to Georgia?"

"At least to the United States."

His heart started beating faster. His thumb traced the line of her jaw. She closed her eyes and nuzzled against it.

"So would you take my calls?"

"I'm in this truck with you, aren't I?"

She was. Even though the light of dawn pinkened the sky, her wide gray eyes had turned dark.

"I know the timing couldn't be worse. I don't know if our schedules can possibly dovetail. But can we try to make time with one another while we're here?" he asked.

"I'd like that. But I don't know how we're going to make that work."

Stay in my room.

He didn't say it. She must have heard him because her eyes went even darker, and her arms twined around his neck. "Do you still take kisses?"

"With you. Only with you."

She was gorgeous. He cupped her face, relishing the softness of her skin beneath his palms. He bent forward, and as gently as possible he slid his lips against hers. She was a treasure that he wanted to tempt into following his lead. Gliding his tongue along her lower lip, she opened with a sigh. He felt her smile.

Who was taking who? Sarah's tongue met his and seduced, beguiled, and heat soared. When had his hands moved? Who cared? God, her ass felt perfect. So round and lush, filling his palm like it had been made for him. He squeezed, and she moaned, pressing her breasts hard against his chest. His goddamn dick was going to burst out of his jeans.

Her nails bit into his nape, and she made mewling sounds. She moved and her leg hit his. He hissed in pain.

"David?"

"It's nothing."

Little nurse arched back from him. Reluctantly, he loosened his grip on her butt and stroked.

"Stop that, I can't think," she protested.

"Who asked you to?"

She pushed out of his arms so she was sitting alone on the bench seat beside him. "What's wrong with your leg?"

"It's bruised."

"What happened?"

"Falling debris from the earthquake. I'm fine. It's better than it was."

"Let me look at it when we get to the clinic."

"Honey, I don't have time. It really is fine. I've been clearing debris for the last two days, and it hasn't gotten worse."

She gave him a considering look. "Okay. But when we're alone together, I'm going to examine it."

"When we're alone together, there are other parts of my body I would prefer you examine."

She laughed and hit his shoulder. "I like you, David Sloane." She kissed his chin. "I think when I'm examining your cock, I can manage to examine your thigh as well."

Pulling her into his arms, he kissed the tip of her nose. "As long as you realize which one takes priority." He buckled them up and started the truck.

CHAPTER FIVE

It took ten solid minutes for Sarah to get her head in the game when she got to the clinic. It was the little girl who asked if her mommy was going to be okay that snapped her out of her euphoric haze. David Sloane sure could pack a punch.

"Lady, my mommy is crying."

"Show me." Sarah gently clasped the little girl's hand and let her lead her to the hole in the back of the clinic to where the young woman was leaning against the outside wall. She was holding a toddler and she was wiping tears off her face. It was clear that it had taken a Hurculean effort to get to this point.

"Good Girl Rosa, you found someone," she gasped. The woman turned to Sarah. "Gringa?"

"Yes, I'm an American," Sarah responded in Spanish. "I'm a nurse." She pulled the little boy from the young mother's arms. Then she saw the problem. Her shoulder was dislocated, and from the way she was standing, there was something wrong with her leg or foot.

"Let me go inside and see if there is someone strong who can carry you inside," Sarah said. Arnie might have been a drunk and a druggie, but at least he'd had a strong back. Of course he needed to be forced to help out.

Asshole.

"Give me Alejandro," the woman demanded softly.

"Let me help you sit down." Sarah eased her to the ground, and then arranged for the toddler to sit on his mother's lap.

"Thank you."

"I'll be right back."

She ducked back into the broken part of the clinic wall. She followed the noise to one of the curtained areas. She found bedlam. There was a teenage boy on a gurney, and a doctor whose hands were wrist deep in his chest. A woman was crying in the corner. There was a small family huddled in the corner, a woman was in the middle, sobbing. The oldest man was clearly stopping her from going to the boy on the operating table.

The three other aid workers were assisting the doctor. Somebody needed to get the family out of the makeshift room, so the task fell to Sarah.

"Please, come with me." She blocked the view from the family. The man that Sarah suspected to be the boy's father threw her a grateful look. He guided his wife out of the curtained cubicle and the two younger men followed. She guided them to the makeshift waiting room, that contained a semblance of a couch.

"Have a seat. I want to assure you that Doctor Fredericks is one of the best doctors I've ever worked with." She just didn't know why he was in a full-blown open chest operation in the clinic and hadn't had the teenager sent to the hospital. It had to be really bad.

"My baby fell on a spike when he was helping move debris," the woman moaned. "He was trying to help."

Sarah crouched down in front of her and grabbed her hands. "As soon as I can, I'll find out what is going on."

"Bless you."

"In the meantime, there is a woman who is hurt and needs help. She's outside and I need assistance bringing her into the clinic."

"Roberto and Esteban will help," she said tiredly. She nodded to the two older boys who stood at attention.

"Thank you," Sarah said and stood up. She motioned to the young men. "Follow me."

"Mama. Mama. Mama wake up." Sarah heard Rosa's shrill voice clearly, and sped up. She ducked through the hole in the wall and found the woman passed out. Alejandro was crawling away in the dirt, she scooped him up. Sarah turned to the two young men.

"Can you pick her up and follow me? Rosa, take my hand. We're going to get your Mama inside and take care of her. It's going to be all right."

"What's wrong with her? Why did she go to sleep?"

"She's tired, Honey." Sarah watched as the boys carefully picked up the woman. She led the way through the hole. She knew there were more gurneys next to the makeshift operating room, so that was where she guided them.

When she got there, she found all of them occupied.

Damn!

"We're going to take her to the sofa where your mom and dad are, okay?" It was either Estaban or Roberto who nodded. As soon as their parents saw them carrying the unconscious woman, they got up so that she could be placed on the couch.

"Give him to me," the older woman said, holding her hands out for Alejandro. Sarah passed over the toddler. She then bent over and checked the young mother's pulse, which was strong. That was when the woman started to rouse.

"What happened?" she asked.

"You fainted." Sarah explained.

She looked around frantically, then relaxed as she spied her children, then she gasped with pain.

"Hold still," Sarah admonished. "I'm going to get you into a triage room as soon one is available and we will get you fixed up." The front door of the clinic opened, and she saw a big man helping a smaller man. The smaller man was holding a compress to his head. It was going to be a busy day.

* * *

Dr. Fredericks finally staggered out of the area where he had been working on Angel. Sarah had arranged for an ambulance to be waiting to transfer the teenager to the hospital. The doctor said there was a good chance that the teenager would survive, barring any infection.

Rosa, Alejandro and their mother, Lisa, were currently huddled in a corner. Sarah had put her shoulder back in its socket and put a cast on her ankle. Lisa explained that her husband had died in the earthquake and she was now waiting for her in-laws to come and pick her up. There were scant supplies, but Sarah had managed to find juice boxes for both of the children, and she handed over the bananas and biscuits that David had forced her to take from the hotel.

When she took a much needed break, Sarah cuddled little Alejandro. His dark brown eyes and wavy hair made her think of David as a child. Then she started to think of what a child of theirs would look like.

Tears welled, but she forced them back. The last time she had thought of dreams like that had been with Matt, and look where that had gotten her. She kissed the top of the little boy's head and handed him back to his mother.

* * *

"Where is he?" David asked again, his voice low, deadly.

The man who had been slouched at the break table shot up and saluted.

"He left yesterday after you and the governor did, we haven't heard from him since."

"Gather every other officer in this building, and have them in the warden's office in three minutes."

"But the warden's office is locked," the man protested.

"It won't be for long."

David turned and walked down the hallway and up the stairs back to the warden's office. The damn building felt like a ghost town. It had taken him ten minutes to find the one ass clown in the break room.

The administrative building, which was separate from the rest of the prison, was still intact after the earthquake. For fuck's sake, the guard at the gate had let David in, believing him when he had shown his military ID. At least the fencing around the perimeter was back up. There were also armed guards in the two towers that were still intact, but he hadn't seen anyone walking the prison yard.

When he got to the door of the warden's office, he saw a man standing outside looking as pissed off as David was feeling. He looked up when he heard David arrive.

"Don't bother knocking, he's not here."

"I know." David gave the door a considering look. Damn it. It would normally be a piece of cake if his leg wasn't still bothering him. Still. He was sick of this shit. He braced and lifted his leg and kicked. Fuck! That hurt. But the door gave way, and he strode through into the office.

"Guess you wanted in." The man chuckled.

"Guess so." David turned on the light, strode around the desk, and started opening desk drawers. Every single one of them was unlocked. For this alone, the man needed to be fired. "Why are you here?" David asked the man.

"To quit."

"Why?"

"It's wrong just to leave a job. My supervisor isn't here. So I was going to tell the warden."

Interesting.

"Yeah, but why do you want to quit?"

"Because the warden and his men are useless," he said vehemently.

"Don't quit just yet. I need your help." David found the drawer with the personnel files. He found the warden's phone number, as well as the numbers of the five men who reported directly to him. He started with the warden. He didn't get an answer. It wasn't until he made his fourth call that somebody picked up.

"This is David Sloane. I've been appointed by the lieutenant governor to take over the apprehension of the escaped prisoners. I'm here at the prison. Where are you?"

The line went dead.

"You're here to help?" the man in the office asked.

"Yes."

"I'm Joaquin Morales. It was my day off when the earthquake hit, but normally I worked on the cellblock where most of the men escaped. We have to find them," he said urgently. "They can't be left on the loose." He slapped both of his hands on the desk and leaned forward. "The warden has been doing nothing to find them. Those men are evil. No woman is safe, and people are going to end up dead."

"Are there are others like you who feel this way?"

"Yes," he said excitedly. "And not just other guards here at the prison either. I'm leaving to lead a manhunt."

"Joaquin, it's a pleasure to meet you. I can arrange things like cell phones, additional vehicles, as well as some members of the police who can be trusted."

"I have eight men."

"Now that I know the warden, and many of his men aren't going to be of any use let's see who is. Gather your team, and bring them back here. I'll call in the officers who will join the hunt. I also know someone else who can get us some volunteers."

He punched in Carmen's number.

* * *

Everybody in the prison yard was sweating, but Bernardo had to be the worst. Finding out your warden had left the country, probably with a bag of drug money, would do that to a lieutenant governor.

"Captain Sloane is in charge of the manhunt." Bernardo grabbed his arm and held it above his head. "I have just promoted Luis Martinez to Warden. He is now in charge of the prison." Bernardo used his other hand to grab Luis' arm above his head. Standing between David and Luis, it was like he was a fight promotor who was declaring everyone a winner. The gathered men cheered.

David looked around, he had ten teams of four men. They would work in twelve-hour shifts, and each team would have a team that it would work interchangeably with. Joaquin would be in charge of one shift, and David the other.

In his gut, he believed many of the convicts were going to be trying to get to the docks, so he put one of the teams there. The rural area was huge, so he put two of the teams in charge of checking the countryside. One team patrolled San Marcos, and one team patrolled the small towns.

When Bernardo finally let go of him, he moved motioned for the team leaders to come forward.

"I want you to check in every hour. Our teams will be working in two twelve hours shifts. The first shift will work with me. The second shift will work with Joaquin. Remember they took weapons from the armory, so we need to consider all of these men armed and dangerous. Joaquin, you and your second shift leaders and men need to go and rest, you will take over in twelve hours."

"I'm good to go now," one man who was part of the second shift said.

"We are doing this by the rulebook," Joaquin said swiftly. "Go home and rest. Your turn will come."

Yep, he'd done the right thing putting Joaquin in charge. David turned to Luis. "Will you be ready when we bring in these assholes?"

Their eyes turned towards construction workers who were maneuvering a steel beam into place on part of the collapsed prison. Even now, a lot of the current prisoners were living four in a cell, instead of the normal two.

"I don't care if I have to chain them to a stake in the prison yard, I'll figure out a way to keep them in place when you bring them to me," Luis growled.

David had read over the files of the escaped convicts, and the idea of Hector Salazar with a steel collar around his neck was very appealing. Luis must have read his mind.

"David, you know some of them have already hurt people."

His teeth hurt as he ground them together. Deep in his gut, he knew that somewhere out there were one or more people in their clutches, and it killed him that they hadn't been looking for these monsters yesterday.

"I know, Luis."

Luis clapped his hand on David's shoulder. "You're going to get them. I trust you."

"Damn right we will," he said catching Joaquin's gaze.

* * *

David had gone with one of the teams into the Las Flores countryside. They had passed a cluster of homes, knocked on each door, and came up empty. An old man at the last house had told them where some other outlying homes were, so the team split up to check them out. David took a young man named Manuel to go with him. Hell, he couldn't be more than eighteen.

Talk about off the beaten path. It seemed like these people wanted to hide from everyone.

"They probably grow marijuana," Manuel said to David's unasked question. It made sense. Even if there weren't prisoners lurking about, chances were the owners of the little homestead weren't going to be happy to have them knocking on their door.

"Let me go first," David said. "You stay back." Smoke curled out of the chimney, and chickens pecked in the front yard, but there were no other signs of activity.

He knocked on the door and waited. Finally, a woman answered. She only opened the door a fraction before demanding to know what he wanted. He explained about the escaped prisoners and asked if she had seen anything. She looked like she was in pain, but she said in a loud voice, that she hadn't seen anything out of the ordinary.

He didn't believe her for even a second. Fear practically seeped from her pores.

"Lady, can I have some water?"

"No. Go away." Her eyes pleaded with him. His neck crawled. He was being watched, and it wasn't Manuel.

"Do you have a cell phone?"

She nodded. He'd been astounded to find out how many people in the rural areas had cell phones, but Bernardo had assured him it was normal. They might not have indoor toilets, but they had cell phones.

"Good. If you see something. Anything. Call the police." She slammed the door. David walked back to Manuel. "This was a waste of our time. Let's go," he said loudly enough for anyone in the house to hear.

He waited until they walked over the rise before taking out *his* phone and calling the others on the team. He told them where to meet. He also called the other four man team that was positioned in the countryside and asked for their location. Four miles, but they could get their hands on a truck.

"Do it," David ordered. He handed the phone off to Manuel so he could provide directions. They were going to need all the back-up they could get.

Then he told Manuel to wait for them, while he circled back through the trees to get another look with his binoculars at the little farmhouse.

There was a small stable, and he saw a horse and a mule. Then he saw something yellow near the foot of the mule. He adjusted the lens. It was a yellow shirt. Dammit, it was a body. Adjusting the lens again, he could make out bloating. The man had been dead for at least two days.

He looked around the backyard, and saw more chickens, then he lifted the glasses so that he could look into the small house. Good, it was a clear view into the kitchen. The woman was not in sight, but he could see a toddler on the floor. The three men seated at the table had on prison uniforms. He swung the binoculars back to the baby and sucked down bile. There was no way one of the men was related to that little boy, not with how scared that woman had been. No, this was a hostage situation.

The woman came into view. She was carrying something, and she put it on the table. One of the men grabbed her and pulled her onto his lap. She struggled.

Don't lady. Just do what they want. Help is on the way.

Another man pulled out a knife and laughed. He pierced the tabletop with it. The woman stopped struggling. They all laughed.

David double checked that his phone was on vibrate, and called the team leader.

"What's the ETA on the other team, Raul?"

"Twenty minutes," the man answered.

"Okay. Follow the GPS to my phone. Do not make any noise. A woman and baby depend on us." He hung up. Damn, he needed a plan. Where he was situated was about one hundred yards from the kitchen window. Could he make the head shots? If he got closer, sure. But not before one of them grabbed the knife and a hostage. They needed a diversion.

His team arrived. He gave them credit, for four men, they were incredibly quiet.

"I'm a sharpshooter," an older man said quietly as he stepped forward. He was holding a well-cared for rifle. He had binoculars hanging around his neck, and it was clear that he had already assessed the situation. David liked him.

He motioned for all the men to huddle in close.

"I see three men in the kitchen, but for all we know, there could be more. There's a dead civilian in the stables and a woman and child in the kitchen. We need a diversion."

"Drugs," Manuel said flatly. The team leader nodded.

"Explain," David demanded.

"I saw marijuana plants as we came over here. It's clear that's what they grow here. Someone pretends to come to the house as a buyer with money. All of their attention will definitely be on the supposed money, not on the woman or the kid."

"Good plan. If at least two men show up at the front, that will force two men to go there, while some of us could go to the back and get the baby and the woman." David nodded, he liked the idea. He turned to the older man with the rifle.

"You'll stay up here. You take out anyone who moves wrong." The man smiled, showing two missing teeth.

These men were impressive. Raul and another one walked up to the front, while David and Manuel crawled down the hill, taking cover in the long grass and shrubs. When they made it to the stable, they stayed still. The sharpshooter would be able to see everything, and he would tell them when to move across the backyard toward the kitchen door.

Yelling pierced the quiet. It was Raul and a man that David assumed was a convict. He could make out the words *drugs* and *money.* Then a shot rang out. He pushed Manuel out of the stable, and the two of them ran toward the kitchen door. Another shot rang out. A baby started to cry. David stumbled, and Manuel grabbed his arm, heaving him up.

Goddamn leg.

"Kitchen! Go! Now!" It was the sharpshooter. David plowed through the door of the kitchen. One of the men who had been sitting at the table had a knife in his hand and was reaching for the baby. As one entity, David and Manuel tackled the man.

Ice. Fire. Pain.

Why wouldn't his arm move to hit the guy? Other hand. He pulled back and slammed his fist into the fucker's mouth.

Crunch.

"You're bleeding."

"Baby. Get the baby," David wheezed.

Another shot.

God, he hurt. He tried to roll over and groaned.

CHAPTER SIX

"He saved them," Manuel said for the third time in three minutes.

"We all saved them," David corrected again, biting back a wave of nausea.

His phone vibrated, and he tried to answer it.

"Don't move," Sarah's voice was strident. He looked up at her, and she looked as sick as he felt. A nurse shouldn't get sick at the sight of blood. He tried to switch the phone to his other hand.

"Goddammit, I said don't move." Her eyes blazed fire.

"I have to take this call."

"Manuel, take his phone and answer it. I need to finish stitching him up." Manuel gave him a pleading look, and David gave the young man his phone.

"Sarah, I'm coordinating things for the next four hours. I need to take those calls," he attempted to explain. When had he ever thought she was hesitant and unsure? This was a woman who would twist off your nuts and shove them down your throat.

"Figure out a solution, because you're benched!" They were nose to nose. He felt his dick twitch, and it wasn't from fear.

"Manuel, call Joaquin and tell him we ran into a bit of a snag, and he'll have to take over a little earlier than anticipated." The kid saluted and then pushed past the curtain to let himself out of the little treatment area in the clinic. There was a curtain because half of the wall was missing.

"Sarah, it's not that big of a deal," he started.

"I'm the one who is now tying up your twenty-seventh stitch. I'm going to say this is a big deal," she said too quietly. All fight had left her now that he'd agreed to rest. Now he could see the fear behind the anger, and it made his heart hurt.

"Are you done?"

She tossed the tools into a stainless steel pan. "Yes, I'm done."

His right shoulder and chest hurt, so with his left hand he picked up her right hand. He held it up in front of their faces. "Your bruised knuckles are also a big deal."

"It's not the same thing at all, you could have been killed," her voice trembled.

Ah, God. Such pain in her voice, and he couldn't even tell her it was going to be all right, because this was a terrible situation, and he didn't know what was going to happen next. He knew this was her worst fear.

"I wasn't. Nor do I intend to be. I'm sorry I scared you." He brought her knuckles to his lips and kissed them.

"Don't try to charm me."

"Would it work?" He gave her his best smile.

She sighed. "Maybe. Probably. That's why I don't want you to try. This is too important. You scared the hell out of me. I know you didn't mean to, but you did."

David closed his eyes. Then popped them open. "Whoa. What did you give me?"

"I gave you a shot for the pain."

"Honey, I need to keep it together. I'm in charge of this manhunt."

"No, you're not. You just put Joaquin in charge. Which as luck would have it, finally dovetails with the end of my shift. So let's get back to the hotel."

Not that they'd be able to do anything with the horse tranquilizer she shot him with.

What the fuck?

"It wasn't a horse tranquilizer."

"Did I say that out loud?"

"Clear as a bell." She helped him off the exam table. She helped him step over the uneven floor on the way to the door. They found Manuel in front of the clinic.

"Did you call Joaquin?" David asked, pissed when his voice came out slightly slurred.

"Yes. He wanted me to tell you that he would call you tomorrow. I stayed so I could drive you to your hotel."

"Could you drive both of us? He was my ride this morning." David watched as Manuel smiled brightly at Sarah.

Of course, he would. What man wouldn't?

"Yes, ma'am. I would be happy to."

David settled into the backseat. He tried to focus on the conversation going on between Sarah and Manuel, but he couldn't. He was too damn tired.

* * *

The phone was ringing, and he groaned in pain. He moved to find it.

"Stop! I'll get it." The bedside lamp turned on, and he got a tasty view of Sarah in his T-shirt as she reached over the side of the bed and groped for his phone. It must have been in his pants.

She handed it to him. Before he could even say hello, Joaquin started talking. He threw off the covers and was standing beside the bed. The pain only mattered because it slowed him down.

"When?" he demanded. Joaquin was garbled. He wasn't making a whole hell of a lot of sense. But one thing was clear. Prisoners had taken over the hospital and were holding Carys and other doctors for ransom, and it was making international news.

"Why are you just telling me now?" It had happened while he had been asleep, and Bernardo had decided to handle things himself.

"Sarah, turn on the TV," David demanded as he started to get dressed. She didn't ask any questions, just found the remote, and stopped on the first channel that didn't have static.

"Oh my God, David, that's the hospital," she cried, pointing to the screen. Then she ran towards the bathroom.

"Tell me everything, Joaquin." David sat down heavily on the side of the bed.

"They're demanding a plane off the island, and ten million US dollars."

"They'll never get that."

"The lieutenant governor called the US Embassy in Panama and your commander. He has also done interviews. He's begging for the United States to give the men whatever they want. Not only are the Doctors Without Borders at risk, but every man, woman, and child in the hospital are now hostages." David saw Sarah come out of the bathroom dressed in the same bloody clothes she had been wearing yesterday when she had stitched him up. Her intent was clear. He dropped the phone on the bed and blocked her exit.

"Let me go," she eyed his shoulder. For the first time he was glad he was injured, knowing that she would have pushed past him otherwise.

"I'm not letting you leave."

"David, I have to get to the hospital."

"And what will you do when you get there?" he demanded.

"I'll figure it out when I'm there." She was getting desperate, he could see it on her face, hear it in her voice.

"Stay with me," he urged. "I need to get to the lieutenant governor's office and find out what he's doing. You can't do anything at the hospital but stand outside. Come with me and we'll see what's being done."

"Please, I'm begging you, let me go to the hospital." Ah shit, she was starting to cry.

He pulled her into his arms. Damn that hurt. She stiffened.

"Stop that. You're hurt." She sniffed and wiped her nose with her sleeve. She yanked up his shirt and looked at his bandage. "Looks okay for the moment." She took a deep breath. "Let me get my supplies."

"Supplies?"

"I brought extra bandages and sutures. I didn't trust you not to rip your stitches." Her eyes welled up again. Her eyes turned to the TV. She watched the picture of the hospital and the Breaking News headline. She grabbed her bag, turned off the TV and turned to him. "Let's go."

* * *

David took one look at Bernardo, and all of his anger left. The man looked like he had aged twenty years since the previous day.

"You should have called."

"You just captured three prisoners and damn near died doing it," the lieutenant governor said quietly. He was seated behind his massive desk, his arms folded in front of him. Carmen was standing over him, she looked like she wanted to cradle him in her arms.

"Tell me the situation and what steps you've taken."

"We think there are ten of them. They've been releasing patients for the last two hours. Two have died because they took them off the machines that were regulating their breathing."

Sarah's fingernails dug into his forearm.

"The others? Where have they been taken? Who's taking care of them?"

Bernardo looked up at her, his expression helpless. "Almost all of our caregivers are in the hospital. Almost all of our medicines and equipment…"

"Haven't you pulled in the personnel from the two regional clinics? They have medicine," Sarah said.

"Yes. But right now I'm more focused on trying to get the rest of the hostages released."

"Carys and the other doctors?" Sarah asked.

"Dr. Adams is the one American doctor. They have actually contacted reporters and told them their ransom demands. They are demanding it of the American government. They are so stupid. America will never give into their demands. Nobody will. These animals must be put down." At last Bernardo seemed to have some life in him.

"What steps have you taken?" David asked again.

"Right now they have us running around handling all of the patients they are releasing. We can't handle anything more. But I have been in contact with the US, they are sending in a team to rescue the hostages."

"Who are they sending?" David asked.

"A Navy SEAL team, Black Dawn." If it had been Army Rangers, then David would have heard of them. SEALs not so much.

"When will they be here?"

Bernardo looked at his watch. "Fourteen hours."

"Okay, then this is what we need to do. Get that damn hospital cleared of patients. Sarah, can your round up the medical personnel we have on the island and get whoever is available to the hotel? We'll make that the new hospital." God bless her, she just nodded.

"Bernardo, you're the face of this island, you'll need to work as the hostage negotiator. Whoever we can get out of that hospital before the SEALs get here, the easier their job will be." David turned to Joaquin. "Do we have a real count of how many bad guys are in the hospital?"

"No. We think there are ten."

"Then we need a real count. That's our first priority. We work with the patients who have been released. We have prison records, and we know the men who escaped. We have them identify pictures. I want to know who the hell is in that hospital," he growled.

Joaquin nodded.

CHAPTER SEVEN

"There's nine."

"Are you positive Joaquin?" The man looked up from the computer screen he had been staring at for the last hour. They were set up in the post office two blocks from the hospital. When David had first arrived on the scene, they had been in an old annex building across the street from the hospital that was used to store old paper patient records. It was one story, and it was obvious the prisoners could pick off the inhabitants.

Now they had someone stationed in the church bell tower that was a story taller than the hospital. It was three hundred meters away, but with a high power scope, it was possible to see into most of the hospital windows. David had been up there an hour ago. The situation was not good at all.

They had released all of the patients and the Las Flores personnel, but it still left them with eight aid workers and nine escaped prisoners. One of the Las Flores orderlies had been assaulted before being released, so it was deteriorating fast inside the hospital. Dr. Adams was the one woman left. She was also the one American. David prayed they wouldn't want to harm her because they would consider her their most essential hostage.

"Joaquin, show me all of the assholes' records. I want to see if there are any weak links we can take advantage of." He glanced at his watch. Three more hours before the SEAL team would arrive. He sat down at Joaquin's desk and they went through the files together.

"It looks like these two hate one another." David put the two photos up side by side. They ran two separate gangs. "It's amazing they're working together." He got up slowly from the desk. Goddamn, his shoulder, and chest hurt, but if he took anything for the pain, he'd be unconscious, and they didn't have time for that shit.

"You shouldn't be up," Carmen said as she tried to hand him a cup of coffee. He waved her off.

"Where's Bernardo?"

"The governor's in that office sleeping," she said pointing to a closed door. "There's another office with a couch. You should take a nap."

David went over to the office that Bernardo was in. He opened the door and stepped in.

"Bernardo?" The man didn't rouse.

"Bernardo?" David shook him.

"What? I'm awake. Are the SEALs here?"

"No, I need to ask you some questions. Come out to Joaquin's desk." David helped the man as he stumbled. He showed him the two pictures. "Which one are you talking to? Which man is making all of the demands?"

"They both are. It's always a three-way conversation."

Got it!

"Bernardo. Now I need you to go back to that annex building and talk to only Salazar through the bullhorn."

"But Molina won't like that. They are both in charge."

"You're going to ignore Molina. You're only going to talk to Salazar. We're going to start some infighting. I want you to say you can only talk to one leader, and you know that Salazar is the one with power."

"Why did you choose Salazar?" Bernardo asked.

"Because it was Molina's man who assaulted the woman. I'm hoping Salazar's gang is better than Molina's."

"They're both animals. It's a bad bet," Joaquin said.

David knew it was true. But it was the only thing he had to go on.

His phone rang. He didn't recognize the number, he assumed it must be someone from one of the manhunts.

He listened.

No.

It wasn't true.

It couldn't be true. David sank against the desk.

"Calm down." He needed the man, no, the boy, to calm down.

"They killed them. They killed them all. They're dead." He was crying so hard it was difficult to understand him. "They butchered them." A deep rock of dread hit the pit of his stomach.

"Who's dead?"

"My papa. My uncle."

Fuck. Fuck. Fuck.

David put the phone on speaker. "Where? Where are you? Are you safe?"

"They called me. They told me to run. We were in the mountains. I hid in a cave with my cousin."

"Who are you? What's your name?"

"Juan."

Too many damn Juans. "Juan who?"

"Juan Hernandez, sir."

"I need you to calm down. Take a deep breath. You and your cousin, are you safe?"

"I think so," came the trembling reply.

"When were your uncle and father killed?"

"They called two hours ago. My cousin went and found their bodies. The other three men were dead too. They were cut up. Why would they do that?"

To make a fucking point. The fuckers were trying to scare the prison guards. Try to get them to stop tracking them.

David put the phone on mute. "Joaquin, can you get them tracked on GPS?"

Joaquin shook his head.

"Why the hell not?"

"Only have the team leader's phones set up to track one another." Damn it! David took the phone off mute.

"Juan, can you tell us where you are?" David kept his voice calm. Reassuring.

"We're two hours from the prison. In the mountains. Can you come and get us?"

David put the phone on mute.

"How old are these kids?" he asked Joaquin.

"Eighteen, same as Manuel," Joaquin explained.

Yeah, but they'd just seen their parents butchered. Now they were scared boys.

David turned to Bernardo. "Call the other team who's out in the countryside, see if they can pick them up. Even if they can't, tell them to be on the lookout for these butchers."

"I have them on the phone right now," Bernardo said, holding up his cell phone.

David thrust his phone to Joaquin. "Talk to the boys. Keep them calm."

He grabbed the phone from Bernardo and quickly told the team leader the situation.

"We're at least fifteen kilometers in the other direction," the man explained. "The roads are a mess with the earthquake damage. It'll take us hours to get to the kids, especially up in the mountains."

Dammit!

"Well make your way there anyway," David ordered the team leader. "We need to stop those killers."

"We're on it," the man answered, then he hung up.

David turned back to Joaquin and motioned for him to mute the phone again. After he had muted the phone with Juan, David asked, "Who do we have at the prison that could get the kids?"

"Nobody good," Joaquin admitted.

Dammit! Think Sloane.

They needed to get to those kids.

"I have an idea." He'd read their files, and they were good. "Riggs and Harrison."

"They're prisoners," Joaquin protested. David gave him a hard look.

"Fine, you're right David, but it'll be better if the lieutenant governor calls Luis and suggests it."

"He's not going to suggest a goddamn thing. He's going to call Luis and tell him those two need to be armed and released. Then they're to be sent out with whatever useless fuck there is who knows the area. Do you hear me?"

Joaquin rubbed the back of his neck, and nodded. "Agreed."

He turned to Bernardo. But it was Carmen who spoke up. She held up her cell phone. "I have the acting warden on the phone. Governor, he's waiting for your instructions." David loved the woman.

* * *

It was déjà vu all over again, here he was at the airport with Carlos and the bus. But this time he wasn't going to be seeing the love of his life, he was going to see steely-eyed professionals who would hopefully save people he had come to know and respect.

Love?

He watched as the plane taxied, and realized that was exactly the right word. Love. He loved Sarah Kyle.

He watched as the men walked down the steps. Warriors. Nothing escaped their gaze. Carlos squirmed under their scrutiny.

The man who came forward carried the mantle of leadership and had a definite air of confidence.

"Captain Sloane?"

"Lieutenant Tyler?" David asked.

"Grayson Tyler. Call me Gray. Let me introduce you to my men." He pointed to the big man who stood beside him. Hell, they were all big men. He had piercing blue eyes that could look right into your heart. "This is my second-in-command, Senior Chief Aiden O'Malley, he's our medic."

"The giant beside him is Jack Preston." Jack nodded. "To the left of him, is Griffin Porter. Then you have Dalton Sullivan, Wyatt Leeds and Dexter Evans."

"I'll brief you on the bus." Gray nodded. They all climbed aboard with their duffels. As soon as they got on board, they checked their weapons.

"If you give us one more hour, I think we can get some of the targets eliminated. These are gang members, and right now there is infighting at the hospital."

"Explain," Gray demanded.

"The two leaders are Salazar and Molinas. They hate each other. They've been working together because they want off the island. All of their demands have been made with both of them on the same phone line. It's clear they don't trust one another. The lieutenant governor has been demanding to talk only to Salazar for the last three hours, saying that he knows he's the leader. We don't have listening equipment, but our man on the bell tower, who can see into the hospital, says they've come to blows."

"That's good." Gray nodded in appreciation. "What are your expectations?"

"We expect Salazar's men to make a move on Molina's men. That should result in fewer men for you to have to eliminate."

"Excellent."

"What about the hostages?" Aiden asked.

"There are eight, all members of Doctors Without Borders. One female and she's an American. They are scattered in different rooms around the hospital. We only have eyes on five of them," David admitted.

"Dammit," Aiden O'Malley muttered.

"It sounds like you've done a good job. Who have you been working with, the local police force?" Gray asked.

"The police force is corrupt. He has very few men. He has done almost everything on his own," Carlos piped up from the driver's seat.

"Is this true?" Gray asked.

"Unfortunately, it is. You won't have a lot of people to rely on. The few good men we do have are securing the perimeter of the hospital. We're using locals for the manhunt."

Gray must have heard something in David's voice.

"What? What happened?"

"We still have thirty-three prisoners at large, and they just butchered five men who were in a search party."

"Fuck," the big guy named Jack said quietly.

"How many men do you have searching for these escaped prisoners?" Gray asked.

"I don't know anymore," David admitted. "After the attack, some of the men have abandoned the search. After the hospital situation is handled, I can get back to managing the manhunt."

The truck lurched as they ran over rubble.

"How did you get involved again?" Gray asked.

"I got here the day of the earthquake. I'm an MP. Two Army NCO's were charged by the corrupt police force for assault. I was here to find out what the hell was going on."

"Our lieutenant governor appointed him the Chief of Police for Las Flores," Carlos said proudly.

"You're a member of the United States Army, right?" Gray asked raising his eyebrow.

"Tell me about it. It's a long fucking story, and I pray to God we can drink a whole hell of a lot and laugh as I tell you about it."

"So do I, Captain. So do I."

CHAPTER EIGHT

"Thank God you're here," Joaquin and Bernardo said in unison. Both of them ignored the seven men behind him and started talking at once.

"Hold up. I can't understand you. Bernardo, you go first."

"Salazar shot Molina and one of his men," Bernardo said excitedly. "It worked perfectly. We're down to seven of those bastards."

"Salazar is the worst," Joaquin warned.

"What's the word on the boys?" David asked.

"Juan called ten minutes ago. He and his cousin can hear the men who killed their fathers."

"If he calls again, tell them to stay off the goddamn phone! Those men will hear them, find them, and kill them." David thought his head would explode.

"I did." Joaquin looked sick. Those boys were going to end up dead unless Riggs and Harrison could get to them.

"Have you contacted Riggs and Harrison?"

"When I called it went straight to voicemail, I got no response to my text," Joaquin explained.

"Good for them. They're maintaining radio or cell phone silence. Maybe that means they're close."

Please, God, say they're close.

A throat cleared behind him.

"Shit. I'm sorry." He turned. "This is Lieutenant Gray Tyler, of the SEAL team Black Dawn. These are his men. This is my team. Joaquin Morales, the Lieutenant Governor Bernardo Lopez and the woman who runs everything, Carmen…" Fuck, he didn't know her last name.

"I'm Carmen Garcia." She gave David a dirty look. "He might not know my last name, but he was smart enough to have me get the blueprints for the hospital. You do speak Spanish don't you?"

"Yes, ma'am." Five of the seven men answered. Shit, another thing David hadn't thought to ask. He needed sleep. He rubbed his shoulder; it was hurting like a son of a bitch.

Shut up Sloane, you can bitch and whine in the next life.

"Ma'am, did Captain Sloane also tell you we would need a map of the city?" Gray asked.

"Of course, he did," she snapped. "I have that as well."

Dammit, he had not thought to ask for a map of the city, only the blueprints of the hospital. But Carmen had him covered. He was going to end up owing her his first born.

They went over to the large counter used by the postal workers and laid out the map of the city. The streets around the hospital, the annex building, and the bell tower were of most interest. Then there were the hospital blueprints.

"The hospital has power, it has generators," David explained.

"Do they have key card entries to doors?" Aiden asked.

"Yes," Carmen answered. "We've collected the ones that have all access."

"Great," Gray said.

"Are you using your police force to keep the reporters out of the hospital?" Gray asked.

"The full use of our police force has been securing the perimeter," Bernardo confirmed.

"You did the right thing," Gray said.

"It was David's idea," Bernardo said proudly.

"When did Salazar's men take out Molina's?" Gray asked.

Bernardo looked at his watch. "Twenty-two minutes ago."

"Let's saddle up boys," Gray said looking at his team.

* * *

David was with Gray at the post office coordinating things, while Dalton, Dex, Wyatt, Aiden, and Jack had made their way in through a causeway connecting the hospital basement and the morgue.

Griff was in the bell tower and had three of the doctors spotted on the third floor, with one of the prisoners. The doctors were tied up against the wall of an office.

Dex texted that he had one aid worker, and two tangos accounted for.

A text came into Gray from Jack. It said that he needed a "Go" and "Fast, or we're going to lose a hostage."

"Shit," Gray said. "Jack has a problem. And I still haven't heard from Aiden." David watched as Gray texted Jack that they needed two minutes. Then Gray turned on Jack's microphone so he could hear what was going on.

"Just walk up and put a gun to her head, you dumb ass," a man yelled in Spanish.

God, they had to be talking about Carys.

Why would they want to shoot her, she was their ticket to freedom?

"I wouldn't do that." A voice said over the radio.

Shit. Was that Jack talking? David looked over at Gray who nodded.

"Drop your weapons or I'll kill you all." Jack's Texas twang was fierce.

Gray and David looked at one another. What in the hell was Jack doing?

"Don't do it. There are three of you and just one of him!" The same man was now screaming.

"Don't forget her. She seems to be on my side, and she has your leader by the balls." They heard a woman's laugh.

What the fuck was going on? This was bad.

"Shoot him!" The man screamed again.

"I'm supposed to take you in and return you to the warden," Jack said. "Otherwise, you'd be dead. Now drop your weapons." Jack's calm voice was impressive. It probably scared the hell out of the men in the room. Hopefully, it gave Carys hope.

"Shoot him!" The man was screaming like a mad man.

They heard a shot from a distance. It didn't sound like it came from Jack or anyone in that room.

Then they heard a lot of loud shots, that did sound like they came from Jack. High pitched male screams were coming through the microphone.

"Dr. Adams are you all right? Carys?" Jack asked the doctor.

Please make her answer. Please say she was all right.

"I killed him. Did I kill him? I didn't mean to." She sounded so sad. So scared. But she was alive.

Thank God, Carys was alive!

"Aiden! You done?" Jack yelled.

"Affirmative, all tangos down." Aiden's voice could be heard over the radio.

"Get to the basement. Dr. Adams is injured."

"Roger."

David and Gray took off at a dead run. Please don't let it be a bad injury, Sarah would be inconsolable if Carys died.

* * *

By the time they got there, Aiden was beside Dr. Carys Adams. She had a shallow cut on her chest, that, thank the good Lord, was not going to need stitches.

"Report," Gray said to Jack.

David looked around the small room in the basement. Three men had been killed by shots obviously fired by Jack. There was a man whose pants were around his ankles with his genitals sliced. Well, that required a little more explanation.

"When I got here, Dr. Adams had a knife to that fucker's balls," Jack pointed at the half-naked dead man.

"How'd she get the knife?" Gray asked.

"You'll have to ask her. I'm just impressed she managed to get it and use it." Jack grinned.

"Yeah, I can get behind that," Gray said.

"Me too," David said. Carys wasn't paying attention to her admirers, it looked like she was in shock.

"Anyway, dickless was yelling at his men to shoot her. But they were all afraid to because they thought they might shoot him by mistake."

"Are you shitting me?" Gray asked.

"Nope. That's the point I showed up."

"Are you sure she's okay?" Gray asked.

Jack grinned again. "Aiden beat off all of her fellow doctors to take care of her. He's going to make sure she's fine physically. I think the trauma is going to take some time. But she's one hell of a tough lady, she'll make it." Jack smiled.

"Where are they going to take her?" Gray asked David.

"To the hotel. We made that into the hospital. Then we'll transfer everybody back to the hospital tomorrow."

As soon as he thought of the hotel, he thought of Sarah. Was she there? Was she all right? Was she tired? When could he see her again? This wasn't the time. He needed to focus on other things. Now that this was done he needed to talk to Joaquin and find out what happened to Juan and his cousin.

"I want to thank you for everything, Gray." David held out his hand.

"I don't suppose you have time for that drink," Gray said.

"Not for a long while," David said. Looking at both Gray and Jack Preston, he said, "I can't thank you enough for everything you did here today."

"David, it is amazing what you have accomplished here."

David looked at Gray in shock. That was high praise coming from a man in charge of SEAL team.

"Thanks."

"I don't know if I'm going to be able to swing this, but I'm going to talk to my commander and see if we can stay and help out until things settle down."

David saw Jack nod in agreement.

"After all, we can't let the Army outdo the Navy." Gray gave a smile.

David laughed, and it felt good.

"You do realize you'll have to report to Carmen," David warned.

"I've had worse commanders."

David felt his gut unclench for the first time in days. Now it was time to find Sarah.

* * *

He couldn't get to the hotel fast enough, and it sure as hell wasn't to sleep. It was an absolute madhouse. Two ambulances and three buses were outside the hotel loading up patients.

It took him twice as long as normal to get out of the truck, and he was damn near hobbling as he made his way from the parking lot to the hotel entrance. Was this what it was going to feel like when he reached eighty? All of the mayhem going on in the lobby was a blur until he saw blonde hair.

"Sarah!" Suddenly he wasn't feeling so old. In less than a second, he was across the floor and had her in his arms. So warm. So soft.

"David." Her flushed face jammed into his neck. She breathed his name over and over. Then he felt her tears. "You saved Carys."

"Where is she?"

"She came in with a medic named Aiden. They're over there." She motioned with her hand to a curtained off corner.

"Is she really okay?"

Sarah looked at him. "I haven't talked to her, not really. But I don't think she's going to be okay for a while. Even if her body is. You know?" David hugged Sarah, and she clutched at him. Then he picked her up.

"Put me down," she finally whispered.

"No. I don't want to."

"I know you don't," she whispered. "But I want to go to our room."

He let her body drift down his until her feet touched the floor. She took his hand and led him to the elevator.

"Stairs," he insisted. She rolled her eyes, then nodded her head.

He opened the door to the stairwell, intent on a kiss, but then saw the herd of people. He was not the only one who thought the elevator was a bad bet. She tugged his hand, and they rushed up to the third floor.

In the room, he saw evidence that she had moved in and breathed a sigh of relief. Then all of his attention was focused on one thing, and one thing only. Sarah Kyle was taking off her clothes. Her shirt was tossed off, and she was unclasping her bra.

"Strip," she demanded. "Shower, then sex."

He laughed and started to take off his shirt and groaned.

"Fuck."

"Dammit, David." Bare chested, she came to him and pushed up his shirt. All thought of pain was gone as he cupped her breasts.

"Stop that, your bandage is soaked through."

"Fuck my bandage." He bent and brought a rose colored nipple to his mouth. Heaven. Her breast was so soft to the touch. Damn. Her nipple pebbled against his tongue, and he was as hard as a rock. Good, he felt her hands at his waist. What?

"You're not unbuttoning me."

"No, I'm pushing you away. Dammit, David, have you popped your stitches?"

"Quit saying 'Dammit', David. Say 'fuck me' David. I haven't popped my stitches. I just did some running and the wound bled." He pushed her towards the bed and sat her down. Then knelt down and untied her boots.

"I should be doing that for you."

"Doesn't matter. We're getting naked. Getting wet. Then you're getting wetter. Then we're going to fuck. Then we're going to make love. Got it?"

Way to go, Sloane.

Her hand cupped his cheek. "I'm already wet." She kissed him.

They finished undressing, and she checked his wound.

"You're right, it's okay. Don't scare me like this again."

"I won't," he lied. She looked at him and nodded. Knowing his words were a lie, but appreciating them anyway.

After a decadent shower, where he indulged in the softness of Sarah's skin, he dragged her to the bed. "God, you're beautiful." He didn't know how many days it had been anymore. Four years, five months and twenty-one days? Hell, he didn't know today's date, all that mattered was that he had her underneath him.

He pushed up on her thigh so that it rested over his arm, opening her to him. He looked down, and saw nothing but a pink, wet welcome and shuddered. He snagged the condom he'd brought from the bathroom and sheathed himself.

"Now. I need you now." Looking up, he saw the same welcome reflected in her stormy gray eyes.

He thrust deep, and she moaned, her smile wide. He knew his was wider. Nothing had ever felt better. He shifted, and her thighs clamped around his hips. They found their rhythm, yearning, reaching.

"Deeper, harder," she demanded.

Perfect. Absolutely fucking perfect. He gave her everything she asked for and reveled in it. Oh God, he felt everything in his body begin to tighten. No, not without her.

Shudders wracked her body and her nails bit into his ass.

"David," she wailed.

He was lost. Nothing had ever felt better.

When he opened his eyes and looked into the soft gray eyes, he realized he'd been wrong. He was found.

* * *

"You need to sleep."

"I can't, baby."

He found clean clothes that Carmen had somehow found for him and started to put them on.

"I'm not talking as your lover. I'm talking as your nurse. Yes, you were wonderful in bed. Frankly, I don't know how you managed it. You need sleep."

Her words were strong, but there was something in her tone of voice…

"Sarah, what's going on?"

"Nothing. Nothing's going on. I told you, you almost died. You need to stay here and sleep."

There it was. He almost died. Could he be more of an idiot? She stood there, her fists clenched by her sides, standing in her panties and bra. He put out his hand and waited. Finally, she took it. He drew her down on the tousled bed beside him.

"I'm not going to die."

"You don't know that. Don't promise me something you can't deliver on." She reached out one trembling hand and traced his bandage. A tear trickled down her cheek.

"My job isn't combat. My job is boring. I do investigations." She continued to trace his bandage. He tipped her chin up, forcing her to look up at him. "You understand that don't you, Sarah? My job is boring."

"You almost died. I couldn't cope if you died." Another tear fell. "Do you have to go?"

"Yeah, I do."

"But the SEALs are here. You told me they're staying. There's Joaquin, can't he work with them?" He willed her to look him in the eye. She finally did, and his heart almost broke.

"Sarah, how often were you in danger when you were in Africa?"

"That's different?"

"Why was it different?" he asked.

"It didn't matter if something happened to me. It matters if something happens to you. I'm in love with you," she cried desperately. He caught her as she flung herself at his chest.

"Ah, baby. I've got you. I promise I will be so careful, it'll be like I'm wrapped in cotton wool. I promise. Now that I have you in my arms again, I'm coming back, nothing is keeping me away."

"Do you promise?" she asked desperately.

He pulled away and stared at her. "I give you my word. Coming back to you is the most important thing in this world." She settled back.

"Oh God, did I hurt your shoulder?"

"Honey, I just worried about hurting you."

"Just come back to me, David. I need you."

"I need you too." He stroked her hair, his other hand drifted down to her breast.

His phone rang.

Dammit!

"You have to get it," she said quietly. "You know you want it to be Joaquin." David rested his forehead against hers for one more ring, then got up.

He answered it and put it on speaker.

"Riggs and Harrison got the boys."

David sagged with relief. "Where are they all now?"

"They're all back at the prison. Harrison didn't want to call, he refused to let anyone make any noise until they got back in case the escaped convicts were around."

"Good man."

"The SEALs arrived, what do I do with them?"

"Get out some maps," David huffed out a quiet laugh.

"Huh?"

"They are going to be the best team you can ask for to find those convicts. Call in our search teams. We're going to redeploy them. The SEALs don't know Las Flores like the natives, so we'll pair them up."

"Make sense," Joaquin said. "When will you be here?"

"I'm leaving the hotel now."

"Lieutenant Tyler said to bring O'Malley with you."

"Will do."

Joaquin hung up, and he looked at Sarah.

"At least you're taking a medic with you. He can help you when your wound starts bleeding or you keel over from lack of sleep." He appreciated the ghost of a smile on her face.

"Hey, why are you putting on clothes? I like you in your underwear," he said trying to keep things light.

"I'm going downstairs with you. I want to check on Carys."

David held out his hand as he opened the door. She took it, and they started down the hallway, skipping the elevators and heading straight for the stairs. Sarah tugged at his hand as he paused at the spot where she had hit Dr. Stanton.

"Don't think about it, David."

That wasn't going to be possible. But he let her lead him away. The idea of the two of them being separated clawed a hole in his gut. He knew how worried she was about him, but he was just as worried about her. The only saving grace was that she would constantly be surrounded by people and should be safe. But he wanted to be the one watching over her.

As they walked into the lobby, it was pandemonium. The lobby doors were wide open, as gurneys passed through towards ambulances. There were still two cur-tained off areas. Amidst all the dark hair of the Las Flores residents, it was easy to spot the blonde giant that was Aiden O'Malley as he hovered over the strawberry blonde doctor. What the hell? David checked his watch. Yep. Three hours ago she had been held hostage, and now she had a stethoscope held against a young woman's chest.

"Do you see them?" Sarah was on her toes, but she couldn't see over the throng of people. David tightened his grip on her hand.

"Follow me."

"Doc, do you mind telling me what you're doing. You need to be resting," David said in his most reasonable tone of voice.

"Yeah, what he said," Aiden growled.

Carys made a shushing motion with her hand, then fin-ished listening to the woman's lungs. She ignored the two men and spoke to Sarah. "How many more in the rural areas need to be brought into the hospital?"

"If they've made it into the clinic and needed hospitalization, I've gotten them there. The problem has been all the people who haven't been able to make it to the clinic. I keep hearing reports of people who have died because of untreated injuries. We need an outreach program. Carys, we need to go to them."

"No way," David said. "Not while there are convicts still on the loose. You are not going door to door looking for earthquake survivors who need care."

"Yeah, what he said," Aiden agreed.

"Don't you have anything original to say?" Carys snapped at Aiden.

"Okay, get to bed. There's a room with your name on it. You just killed a man and were covered in your blood and his. You're still shaky." Aiden gently clasped her wrists in his hands so that they could all see her hands tremble. "If you'd give me that damn stethoscope, I'd find your heart still racing. You're white as a sheet. You need to rest for a couple of hours, or better yet, have some food and go to sleep for the night."

"I didn't ask for a monologue." Shit. She was shocky. That sounded like she was pouting.

"Dr. Adams," the SEAL said in a soothing tone.

"Carys," she corrected petulantly.

"Carys. He's right," David interjected. "You were the one who insisted your people rest the first day you landed. I really respected that." She was on the fence. He turned to Sarah.

Come on baby, bring it home.

"Carys, if I was to check your blood pressure right now, what would I find? Let's go get some food. You and I can talk about the outreach plan. Then you can get a little bit of rest while I take over down here."

"Fine," she huffed. "Since I was triple-teamed. Where are you two going?" she asked David and Aiden.

"We have to go to the prison. They're coordinating the manhunt for the remaining prisoners."

"Are they as dangerous as the…" Carys' voice trailed off.

"They're all bad," David said grimly.

"Go get your food, Carys. When you're figuring out your outreach program, factor in military personnel going with you," Aiden warned.

"You too, Sarah, and it will be me." There was no way he was leaving her safety in anyone else's hands.

"Same goes, Carys," Aiden said emphatically. David looked over at the big SEAL. The man worked fast.

Sarah was smirking, and she looked adorable. He pulled her into his arms, loving how easily she wound her arms around his neck. His beautiful gray-eyed nurse. Her lips molded to his and everything around him fell away, just Sarah remained.

"Captain." Okay, Aiden was still here.

David lifted his head, admiring her wet lips. One last quick kiss. She carefully pushed at his uninjured shoulder.

"Stay safe," they said in unison and laughed.

"Okay, Aiden. Let's go."

CHAPTER NINE

"I'll go to my room, as long as you go with me and tell me what is going on with you and that big hunk of a guy," Carys said as soon as they were alone.

Sarah laughed. It would be good to talk to her friend. "Same goes, it seems like you made a friend pretty fast."

"The SEAL?" Carys asked.

"His name is Aiden," Sarah corrected. "He seemed pretty damned protective."

"I think it's in their DNA." Carys walked slowly towards the stairs.

"Let's take the elevator," Sarah suggested. Carys just rolled her eyes and continued towards the stairs. Sarah laughed again. Despite the horror of the last twenty hours, Carys wouldn't let herself be bested. But Sarah was going to kick her ass and ensure that she got some rest, *and* some professional care. They trudged up the stairs to the room that Carys was sharing with Alena, who was busy at one of the clinics.

"You don't have to babysit me," Carys said when they got to her room. Sarah didn't say anything, she just followed her friend into her room. As soon as they stepped in, she wrapped Carys into a hug. The doctor stiffened. Sarah held on for long moments, waiting. She felt a deep shudder, and finally heard a wrenching sob.

Sarah murmured words of comfort and stroked her friends hair.

"I should be stronger," were the first words Carys said.

"Dammit Carys, I'm going to shake you," Sarah said through her own tears. She maneuvered them to the bed, and got Carys to sit down.

"I need to get clean." Carys yanked at the shirt she was wearing and it got tangled as she tried to pull it over her head.

"Let me," Sarah coaxed. She could see the blood caked on her friend's pale skin as she pulled the shirt off her. As soon as it was off, Carys sprung off the bed and rushed to the bathroom. Sarah followed and held her hair as she threw up in the toilet. When nothing was left, wounded eyes looked up at her.

"Can you help me into the shower?"

"Of course. Then you have to rest."

"No, there's too much to do." Carys was resolute. "I had my mini-breakdown. I'll have a full-blown meltdown when this disaster is cleaned up."

"I won't allow it. I'll tie you to the bed," Sarah growled.

Carys laid her hand on Sarah's shoulder.

"What would you do if the roles were reversed? Be honest."

Sarah looked inside herself. "I'm not sure I'm as strong as you."

"You're stronger, my friend." Carys pushed up from the floor and Sarah helped her into the shower.

* * *

When David arrived at the prison, a lot had been accomplished. Joaquin was finished briefing Gray and his men on the terrain and the convicts who remained at large. Riggs and Harrison were safely back with the young men, and all but six of the men who were going to still help with the manhunt had arrived back at the prison.

"Joaquin is a good man, you really lucked out," Gray said when he and David had a moment to themselves.

"I agree. What's your assessment of Riggs and Harrison?"

"I haven't had enough interaction with them to tell. But I read over their records, and I liked how they handled themselves to get those two kids. Damn shame about their fathers." Gray must have seen the guilt on David's face.

"Stop it. You've done a hell of a job in a terrible situation. You've had to trust that the locals knew what they were doing."

"I appreciate what you're saying, but it still happened on my watch."

Gray nodded, respect evident in his eyes.

"How do you want to play this? I know these are your men. I don't want to be the one giving orders," David said. "What's more, you have a lot more tactical experience."

"The men of Las Flores look to you as their leader. I'll lay out the plan and assign my men, but you can assign the locals to their tasks."

"Sounds good."

They went back to the warden's old office where everyone was gathered.

"Joaquin, what's keeping the men we're waiting for?"

"Their truck broke down. They'll be here in an hour."

"Okay, we'll get started without them."

David looked around the room. There were eighteen residents of Las Flores gathered along with the seven SEALs, him and Joaquin.

"Lieutenant Tyler is going to introduce his team, and then explain our plan. Joaquin and I will assign you men to different groups, paired with different Navy SEALs." David smiled to himself when the Las Flores men perked up at the term Navy SEAL, it seemed even here in Las Flores they had heard of the elite team of soldiers.

Bernardo had also been helpful in his efforts to stop the convicts. There was now a tip line set up, so they would not be flying blind. Carmen's daughter was coordinating the project and alerting the manhunt teams when a tip seemed to have merit.

It was agreed that Joaquin would coordinate things from the prison. Luis, the acting warden, had been disgruntled at first. David had explained to him that his job was too big to care for another monumental task.

"Luis, you're already trying to rebuild a prison, keep riots from happening, and hire new guards. It's too much to ask of you to do one more thing." David's words had pacified him.

With the seven SEALs, Riggs, Harrison, and David, they had ten teams. O'Malley got a call.

"Gray, we have a problem."

"What?"

"That was Carys, she said that she received information that there were two kids hurt at a small farm about fifteen clicks from one of the clinics. She intends to go out and get them to the hospital."

"Yep, that's a problem. Do what you need to do."

David's skin crawled. "Let me guess, she's not going alone."

"Nope," Aiden said. "Your woman is going with her."

"Dammit! I told her to call me."

"You're not raising her right." Aiden smirked. David's palm itched. Then his phone rang.

"David, it's me." His world settled.

"Wait for us. I'll be there in an hour."

"I don't think they have that long. Somebody got a cell phone to them. We talked to someone on site. They're in real trouble. They need immediate triage."

"Let Aiden go, he's a medic." He heard her talking to someone. He couldn't make out what they were saying.

"It's in the wrong direction. You'll have to meet us there."

"Don't you leave without us." He heard Aiden saying the same thing. It was stupid. The leader inside of him screamed that he and Aiden shouldn't both leave, but fuck that. He was going, and something told him that Aiden would be going too. So be it.

Phones to their ears, they grabbed their weapons and headed outside. David pointed to his truck.

"Hang up your phone, O'Malley." Aiden scowled but did as he was told. David did the same thing and handed his phone to the man.

"What do I do with this?" he asked as he took the phone. David started down the road as fast as he could, even though it was a rut-filled mess.

"I can track Sarah on GPS. We have that arranged on a bunch of different specific targets." He saw the man grin.

"They're already moving."

"Of course, they are."

* * *

"My God," Aiden breathed as they pulled up to what must have been a house at one point. They parked beside the jeep the women had used. An elderly man stepped over a pile of rubble as he headed toward them and he looked sick.

"Who are you? Where are the women who drove the jeep?" Aiden demanded.

"What?" the old man was dazed. David scowled at Aiden.

"Hello, sir. Do you live here?"

"My grandchildren…" He waved his hand toward the crumbling house.

Aiden pushed past the man and stepped through the ruined doorway.

"Sir, can you tell me what happened?" David asked.

"My little angel is dead. But my daughter she will not accept it. She just holds and rocks her while her other two children, Oscar and Pira, suffer."

David shook his head. He couldn't imagine the woman's pain. "Where's the person who reported this?"

"He left. He's gone to look for more victims."

"Stay here, I'm going to see if I can help." David went into the house. It was quiet. Too quiet. The ceiling was missing. He saw an opening that led through the kitchen, and there were two rooms. One contained a bed, but had no people, the other had all the people.

There were no blankets covering their battered little bodies, just underwear. He guessed the one in the pink panties was a girl. She couldn't have been more than five, and her legs were at awkward angles. There wasn't a wound, but her chest was caved in.

The little boy was in Spiderman underwear with a bone jutting from his broken arm. Same with his right leg. He was writhing around and moaning. The mom was just as the grandfather said, sitting in a chair, rocking her dead infant.

Carys knelt next to the little girl, she had a grim look on her face and a stethoscope to the little girl's chest.

Sarah was kneeling next to the little boy. She looked up at David, her expression determined. But beneath the determination, he could see her heart aching. Breaking.

The little girl gasped. Then seized. Blood trickled from her mouth. David watched in horror. He looked at the mother. Her rhythm didn't change, she kept rocking her baby as if nothing was happening. As if her other daughter wasn't dying right in front of her eyes.

David looked helplessly at Carys, Aiden, and finally at Sarah. She shook her head, tears in her eyes. The wounds, what he'd seen, he'd known. It was amazing the child had still been alive when they had come through the door.

"We need to get the boy splinted," Aiden said as he put his hand on Carys' shoulder. She wiped the blood away and closed the girl's eyes. She nodded at Aiden. David watched as the three of them worked to get the boy taken care of.

The old man came in and explained that the man had returned with three other local men. David went out and met with them.

"I know Margaret," one man said. "I was friends with her husband. I am sorry it took me so long to get here." He looked down at the dirt, then back up at David. "We will take care of her."

"We're going to take her son with us. We will be able to care for him."

"He will be well?" the man said hopefully.

"Yes, we think so," David answered.

"Thank God," the man said fervently. They all turned to see Aiden carrying the small boy out of the house. He placed him in the back of the jeep, where they had made a pallet for patients.

"We're following you," Aiden said to Carys.

"Thank you," the man said to them.

"You're welcome."

CHAPTER TEN

It was a week after the little girl had died, each night David held her in his arms and comforted her if she cried. Tonight, he'd been the one to wake her. He had to leave again.

Sarah sat up, unconcerned that the sheet fell down to her waist, baring her breasts.

"Is everything okay?" As soon as the words were out of her mouth, she realized how stupid they were. "Scratch that. Will you need a nurse?"

David sat down beside her as he pulled on his boots. When he was done, he pulled her into his arms. "With Gray leading this op, the only medical assistance that might be needed will be the clinic personnel at the prison for the convicts."

She wanted to ask if the SEALs were so good, why did David need to go, but she kept her mouth shut. This was his job. For now.

He must have seen the question in her eyes. "The good news is, this is almost done, Gray's pretty sure this is the last group of prisoners."

"More of Molina's men?" she asked.

She could see him consider lying, finally he nodded.

"Be safe," she whispered.

"Always, I have you to come home to."

He dove in for a deep kiss. She got lost in the sensation. His taste, and urgency swept her away into a world of bliss. Finally David lifted his head. "Keep my place. I'm going to want to finish where we left off."

She nipped his chin, and he laughed.

"I love you Sarah Marie."

"I love you David Allen."

She watched as the door closed behind him.

She pulled up the covers and curled into a tight ball in the bed. Her body started to quake.

"Don't die. Don't die. Don't die. Don't die."

She jammed the heels of her hands into her eyes, trying to stem the flood of tears.

She'd loved Matt, she really had. But it had been a girl's love. It had been young love. She had given everything she could at that age.

But now?

Now, David was half of her soul. He was her world.

"Please God. Please God. Please God."

Hearing those last few words, she calmed.

She'd been given the gift of David Sloane, and that was a blessing, in and of itself. He was amazing, and she needed to hang on to that, not worry about something that might or might not happen. Her breathing calmed. She was going to hold on tight for as long as God and the Universe chose to give him to her. That's all she could do. And she would be grateful.

Sarah smiled. Her heart felt lighter.

She got up from the bed, and went to the bathroom and cleaned up. When she came back to the bed, she could breathe again, and she grabbed David's pillow and sucked in his smell, reveling in his scent. The man she loved. The man she was going to love all of her life.

* * *

For the next two weeks, the island of Las Flores slowly emerged from its devastation. Day after day more prisoners were captured as Gray and his teams worked. Aiden and David worked primarily with Carys and Sarah, but occasionally with other aid workers who went out on the Outreach program to bring in the injured. David was relieved none of the other visits had been as bad as that first. There had been a couple of nights when Sarah would wake up crying, and he would rock her back to sleep.

He talked to his commander. They were down to the last eleven prisoners, so he would soon be going home. Gray had a similar talk with his superiors. He figured they had maybe another week on the island.

Trudging back to the hotel, he looked at Sarah. She smiled back at him. This had been one of the good house calls. A woman had given birth. It had been a breech birth, and Sarah had said that they couldn't take her in the jeep to the hospital. She also said it was complicated. He knew that breech was bad, but it had turned out well—after thirty hours.

God, he was tired, but Sarah looked like she was ready to go dancing.

"Did you see him, he looked like a linebacker. I should say a football player. I mean a soccer player type of football player." She was babbling. He stopped her, and right there in the lobby he kissed her. Hard. She grabbed him and grinned into the kiss. It was a happy and passionate kiss. What a great fucking flavor.

"Get a room!" He tucked her under his arm and turned to glower at Carmen.

"What are you doing at the hotel? I thought your home had been repaired."

"Bernardo wanted me to talk to the hotel about arranging a party for all of you. You'll be leaving soon, and he wants to thank you. I even tracked down Lola and her family for Bobby Harrison." David smiled. "Don't tell him, though, it's a secret." He was really going to miss Carmen.

He looked at Sarah. She had tightened up at Carmen's words.

He tugged Sarah toward the stairs. Even after all this time he still didn't feel good about the elevators. Let's face it, even though the electrical grid was fine, he wouldn't be taking elevators until he was back in the states.

As soon as they got into the room, she turned to him, grabbed at his T-shirt, and tugged it over his head. His bandage was gone, and so were the stitches. She traced the healing flesh.

"Are you feeling better now, Honey?"

"What?"

"Are you feeling safer? Are you beginning to trust that I won't leave you?" Her pretty gray eyes turned misty. She nodded.

"I'm sorry I was so scared."

"There's nothing to feel sorry about. You had perfectly valid reasons to be scared. But this was an extraordinary set of circumstances. I told you, I lead a very boring life."

"There is nothing boring about you, David Sloane."

"What about you? Are you planning on living a boring life, Sarah Kyle?"

"Yep, I already told Carys that when this is all over, I'm going back to the US." He thought his face might split in half with how big his grin was. "I don't want us to break up." She looked up at him. "We *are* in a relationship, right?"

"Make no mistake. This is a relationship. As soon as we get back to the states, and I get to a jewelry store, this is going to get as permanent as possible. I want you in my life permanently, Sarah. I know what it's like without you, and I don't want that ever again."

He held his breath. She searched his face.

"You're serious, aren't you?"

Screwed that up, didn't you, Sloane?

"Sarah Marie Kyle, will you marry me?"

"Do you love me?"

"Oh honey, I love you so much it hurts. I'm sorry, I should have said that first. See, I'm a dumbass. I love your beautiful heart that wants to help heal the world. I love your first class brain that runs circles around mine. I love your body that knocks me off my axis. Do you love me? Will you marry me?"

"I love you. I've probably been in love with you since Fort Lewis. I've just been afraid. Marrying you would make all my dreams come true."

Finally. Four years, six months and four days. That's how long it had taken for his dreams to come true.

EPILOGUE

Aiden O'Malley did his best to relax in the small straight back chair that barely contained his frame with little Oscar perched on his lap. The boy's mother wasn't at the wedding, but according to the little boy's aunt and uncle she was improving.

Looking around, it seemed like she was the only one who wasn't here. Meanwhile almost the entire population of Las Flores had shown up for Bobby Riggs and Lola Hernandez's wedding. But he'd bet his left nut that it was really to see David Sloane. That man was their hero.

The little boy whimpered and Aiden repositioned the child's leg so he would be more comfortable in his sleep. Oscar sighed and snuggled closer. Aiden picked up his beer from beside the chair and settled back as best he could and perused the activities.

The dance floor was jammed packed. The band was alternating between Latin and American music. He saw his lieutenant standing next to Luis and Carlos. They were probably talking about security. Shit, Gray needed to learn how to let his hair down, especially considering how many pretty girls were sending looks his way. He should take a page out of Dex's book. Now that boy was doing just fine out there with the senoritas.

"Can I have your attention!" Carmen bellowed. Then she repeated her demand in English.

Dammit, Carmen better not wake up Oscar.

"I want to thank Bobby and Lola for letting us use their happy event to celebrate the resilience of Las Flores. Nothing will ever keep us down!"

A cheer went up.

Oscar cuddled closer but didn't wake up. Aiden smiled.

"Bernardo, come up and talk to your people." She gestured to the man in the flamboyant suit who looked years younger than he had the last time Aiden had seen him.

"Why?" the now Governor called from the dance floor. "Everyone knows you're in charge."

Everyone roared with laughter.

"David Sloane, you come up and talk!" Carmen commanded.

"No habla Español." David shouted from his spot on the dance floor.

More laughter.

"Okay, I'll speak," Carmen said.

"Big surprise." Bobby Riggs yelled out.

"We have had our time to mourn. Now is our time for joy. Once again we will enjoy our place under the sun, and it is because of the men and women here who are heroes." Carmen's voice broke. "So many of you risked your lives and I thank you. But the man I will always be grateful for is David Sloane."

She raised her glass of champagne as thunderous applause broke out.

Still little Oscar remained asleep.

Thank God.

Bernardo helped Carmen off the stage, and pulled her into his arms for a dance, as the band began to play 'Feeling Good'.

Aiden grinned as he saw Bernardo dip in for a kiss at the same time that David claimed one from Sarah.

The only thing missing was Carys Adams. She'd held it together magnificently until the end of her assignment. He'd tried to help her come to terms with her trauma, but he and Jack were the last people she wanted to see after leaving Las Flores. According to Sarah she was even keeping her distance from her. She'd immediately re-upped for a solitary assignment in the back of beyond.

He was damned if he was going to let that stand. She'd become a friend. She was one of the good ones. He didn't know when, or how, but one day he would find a way to help her get her life back on track, and she would never know he had anything to do with it.

* * *

Out of the corner of his eye David saw Carmen and Bernardo embrace and he tipped his chin so that Sarah would look over.

"Oh," she sighed. "That makes me happy."

"I arranged it just for you, Mrs. Sloane. Keeping you happy is my job." He smoothed back her hair, relishing the opportunity to touch her, caress her.

"You do it well." She pressed closer, and he gloried in the feel of her body against him, their child nestled between them.

"David?" she whispered softly. It was like they were in their own little bubble. They might be surrounded by people, but only their family and their song existed.

"Hmmm?" God, he could lose himself, looking into those big gray eyes.

"Thank you."

"For what?"

"Making me whole again. Making my dreams come true." She was serious. How could she be serious, when she was the one who had made him whole?

He did the only thing possible, he bent down and took a kiss. The feel of her, the taste of her, everything that was Sarah swept through him, making him complete.

It had been six months and eighteen days since she had agreed to be his wife. He would never forget the day she had made his dream come true.

The End.

BIOGRAPHY

Caitlyn O'Leary is an avid reader, and considers herself a fan first and an author second. She reads a wide variety of genres, but finds herself going back to happily-ever-afters. Getting a chance to write, after years in corporate America, is a dream come true. She hopes her stories provide the kind of entertainment and escape she has found from some of her favorite authors.

Keep up with Caitlyn O'Leary:

Facebook: http://tinyurl.com/nuhvey2
Twitter: http://twitter.com/CaitlynOLearyNA
Pinterest: http://tinyurl.com/q36uohc
Goodreads: http://tinyurl.com/nqy66h7
Website: http://www.caitlynoleary.com
Email: caitlyn@caitlynoleary.com
Newsletter: http://bit.ly/1WIhRup
Instagram: http://bit.ly/29WaNIh

BOOKS BY CAITLYN O'LEARY

The Found Series
Revealed, Book One
Forsaken, Book Two
Healed, Book Three
Beloved, Book Four (Spring 2017)

Midnight Delta Series
Her Vigilant SEAL, Book One
Her Loyal SEAL, Book Two
Her Adoring SEAL, Book Three
Sealed with a Kiss, A Midnight Delta Novella, Book Four
Her Daring SEAL, Book Five
Her Fierce SEAL, , Book Six
Protecting Hope, Book Seven
(*Seal of Protection & Midnight Delta Crossover Novel
Susan Stoker KindleWorld*)
A SEAL's Vigilant Heart, Book Eight
Her Dominant SEAL, Book Nine (February 2017)

Black Dawn Series
Her Steadfast Hero, Book One

Shadow Alliance
Declan, Book One
Cooper's Promise, Book Two
(*Omega Team and Found Crossover Novel
Desiree Holt KindleWorld*)

Fate Harbor Series Published by Siren/Bookstrand
Trusting Chance, Book One
Protecting Olivia, Book Two
Claiming Kara, Book Three
Isabella's Submission, Book Four
Cherishing Brianna, Book Five

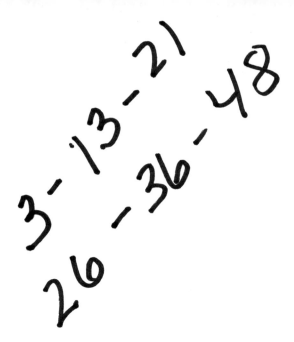

3 - 13 - 21

48

26 - 36 -

Made in the USA
Columbia, SC
12 May 2021

37793491R00078